"SEX IS THE ONLY THING THAT'S GOING TO KEEP ME SANE, DANNY!"

Her arms wrapped even tighter around my neck. Her thighs pressed against mine, her pelvis bumped into mine, and despite myself, things began to stir.

"You have to understand me, Danny! If I don't have you right now, I'll wind up walking up the wall!" Her pelvis screwed more tightly into mine. Her hands fluttered down my back to my buttocks. She pulled them hard against her. I could feel the small yielding area between her legs against my crotch.

"Okay," I said huskily as I gazed at her coral-colored nipples lifting in tumescence, the soft deep curve of her belly, and the tangled bush of blond hair that ranged down the gentle slopes between her legs.

"Thank you," she said softly. "You won't regret it, Danny," she added, already leading me toward the bedroom. . . .

D1715297

SIGNET Thrillers by Carter Brown

- ☐ CATCH ME A PHOENIX (#Q5910—95¢)
- ☐ A CORPSE FOR CHRISTMAS (#Q6153—95¢)
- ☐ THE CORPSE (#Q6468—95¢)
- ☐ THE DAME (#Q6402—95¢)
- ☐ THE DEADLY KITTEN (#Y7152—$1.25)
- ☐ THE DESIRED (#Q5985—95¢)
- ☐ DONAVAN (#Q6033—95¢)
- ☐ DONAVAN'S DAY (#Y6716—$1.25)
- ☐ THE DREAM MERCHANT (#Y7031—$1.25)
- ☐ THE EARLY BOYD (#Q6321—95¢)
- ☐ THE HAMMER OF THOR (#Q6496—95¢)
- ☐ HOUSE OF SORCERY (#Y6755—$1.25)
- ☐ THE IRON MAIDEN (#Q6425—95¢)
- ☐ LONG TIME NO LEOLA (#Y6684—$1.25)
- ☐ NEGATIVE IN BLUE (#Q6220—95¢)
- ☐ NIGHT WHEELER (#Q6103—95¢)
- ☐ NO BLONDE IS AN ISLAND (#T5835—75¢)
- ☐ NUDE WITH A VIEW (#Q6068—95¢)
- ☐ PHREAK-OUT (#T5636—75¢)
- ☐ THE PLUSH-LINED COFFIN (#Y6904—$1.25)
- ☐ REMEMBER MAYBELLE (#Y6995—$1.25)
- ☐ RIDE THE ROLLER-COASTER (#Y6804—$1.25)
- ☐ THE SAVAGE SISTERS (#Y6871—$1.25)
- ☐ SEX TRAP (#Q6515—95¢)
- ☐ SO MOVE THE BODY! (#T5704—75¢)
- ☐ SO WHAT KILLED THE VAMPIRE? (#Y6549—$1.25)
- ☐ THE STAR-CROSSED LOVER (#Q5940—95¢)
- ☐ UNTIL TEMPTATION DO US PART (#Y6840—$1.25)
- ☐ WHEELER DEALER! (#Y6646—$1.25)
- ☐ WHEELER FORTUNE (#T5795—75¢)
- ☐ WHO KILLED DR. SEX? (#T5744—75¢)

THE NEW AMERICAN LIBRARY, INC.,
P.O. Box 999, Bergenfield, New Jersey 07621

Please send me the SIGNET BOOKS I have checked above. I am enclosing $_____(check or money order—no currency or C.O.D.'s). Please include the list price plus 35¢ a copy to cover handling and mailing costs. (Prices and numbers are subject to change without notice.)

Name_____

Address_____

City_____State_____Zip Code_____

Allow at least 4 weeks for delivery

The Pipes Are Calling

by
CARTER BROWN

Ⓢ
A SIGNET BOOK
NEW AMERICAN LIBRARY
TIMES MIRROR
in association with Horwitz Publications

© 1976 BY HORWITZ PUBLICATIONS, A DIVISION OF
HORWITZ GROUP BOOKS PTY. LTD. (HONG KONG BRANCH),
HONG KONG, B.C.C.

Published by arrangement with Alan G. Yates

SIGNET, SIGNET CLASSICS, MENTOR, PLUME AND MERIDIAN BOOKS
are published by The New American Library, Inc.,
1301 Avenue of the Americas, New York, New York 10019

FIRST SIGNET PRINTING, OCTOBER, 1976

1 2 3 4 5 6 7 8 9

PRINTED IN THE UNITED STATES OF AMERICA

The
Pipes
Are
Calling

Chapter One

~~~~~~

Her name was Melanie Rigby, she said. She was around six feet tall in her low-heeled shoes, and oozing vitality out of every pore. Her thick blond hair tumbled down around her shoulders, her eyes were a deep violet color, and her broad mouth had an overhung lower lip that more than hinted at a barely contained sensuality. She was wearing a blue silk shirt that fit real snug across her deep breasts, so her firm nipples made impressive indentations in the thin fabric. The blue jeans were stretched tight across her bountiful hips, faithfully tracing the slight bulge of her venus mound, and her rounded thighs were taut. Gripped between them in a scissorlike hold, in the last throes of sexual rapture, I figured a man could simply die of ecstasy.

"They tell me you're a private detective who's just swapped the East Coast for the West Coast, and settled down right here in little old Santo Bahia," she said. "Is that right, Mr. Boyd?"

Her voice was deep-pitched and kind of melodious. For a moment there, I imagined it saying more intimate things. A hell of a lot more intimate things. Like

... ah ... I quickly ran one or two of them over in my mind.

"Is that right, Mr. Boyd?" she repeated.

"That's right, Miss Rigby," I said.

I turned my head a little so she got the left profile, which is pure perfection. She didn't faint right there on the spot, but only because she was a big, strong girl, I figured.

"You mind if I sit down?" she said.

"Help yourself," I said with great courtesy.

She sat down in the visitor's chair, crossed her legs, which made the bulge contract a little, then looked at me. By way of a contrast, I gave her the right profile, but she didn't scream out in ecstasy, or anything. I just hoped she wasn't frigid.

"It's Mrs. Rigby, incidentally," she said.

"Oh," I said, with a distinct lack of enthusiasm.

"You've worked here before," she said. "In Santo Bahia, I mean."

"Three, maybe four times," I agreed.

"You know what it's like," she said. "A resort town. Hotels and motels, antique shops and tea shops, and not forgetting our beautiful beaches, of course. Then there are places with names like Sublime Point and Paradise Beach, and if you get bored with the scenic wonders, there's always our fascinating country club."

"I know," I said.

"Not too much choice of activities for the local population," she said. "After they've finished ripping off the tourists, I mean."

"Is that right?" I said patiently.

"Well, they do screw around a lot," she allowed, "but that's a typical small-town syndrome. I mean the usual thing—a bit of wife-swapping here and there, Saturday night orgies, drugs, incest, church on Sunday—you name it. In all, a sleepy, God-fearing little community."

"Promises well," I said, giving her one of my lascivious looks. "And what about you, Mrs. Rigby?" I asked politely. "Are you right there in the thick of it?"

"Melanie," she said, "and I'm not sure what you mean, Mr. Boyd."

"Danny," I said. "I mean. . . ." I gestured helplessly. "Well I mean . . ."

"Maybe another time we can have a long talk about whatever it is you mean," she said, "Danny."

"I just love the social chitchat," I said. "Did you have anything else on your mind?"

"I have to meet my husband tonight."

"You'd like me around to make the introductions?"

"We're about to be divorced," she said, "so it'll be a purely business discussion. What with the communal property laws of California, and all, I'm going to bleed him white and he knows it. So he's asked me to meet him at a little old log cabin up in the hills that belongs to the both of us. Or used to belong to the both of us. It's going to belong to me real soon now." She smiled, revealing flawless teeth. "I'm a little nervous, Danny."

"You don't look nervous," I said.

"Broderick could make me feel nervous even when we were happily married," she said wryly. "He makes me feel a hell of a lot more nervous now we're about to be divorced. Broderick is a man with a very quick temper."

"Your husband?"

"About to be my ex-husband," she said. "I mean, why can't we talk it over at dinner right here in town someplace? But he insists we meet at the little old log cabin way up in the hills with nobody else around.

3

The nearest neighbor is at least a half mile away. It makes a girl feel nervous, Danny. Like I need support; a friendly hand at my elbow. The comforting friend at my side who, just by being there, will remove any thoughts of mayhem that could be lurking in dear old Broderick's mind."

"You want me to go with you," I said cleverly.

"Just for company," she said. "It shouldn't take more than four hours from start to finish." She smiled again, and once again I was dazzled by her teeth. "It's no big deal for a guy like you just out of Manhattan, and I know it. Look on it as a favor, Danny. This could be the start of a beautiful new friendship. I'll pay for your professional help, of course. A couple of hundred dollars, if that's enough?"

"It sounds real generous for a night's work," I told her.

"Thank you," she said. "I'm beginning to feel a lot better already."

"You want me to pick you up?"

"I'll pick you up," she said. "Say here, around seven-thirty. I know where we're going, so it'll make things easier if I drive. And you don't need to wear anything formal, there'll only be the three of us. Okay?"

"See you at seven-thirty, Melanie," I said.

She got up out of the chair and walked toward the door. Her bottom, tightly encased in the blue jeans, bounced with a kind of lithe tautness that made me wonder whatever had gone wrong with her marriage. No way could she be frigid, so maybe the problem had been with dear old Broderick. Then the door closed in back of her and I stopped speculating. It was around four in the afternoon and I now had a client, so I could stop working for the rest of the day.

The office was above one of the antique shops just off the main drag. A two-room apartment went with it, which was comfortable, and also big, enough to swing a girl around by her hair without knocking lumps of plaster off the walls. I changed into swim trunks and collected a beach towel, then put on some cheaters and walked to the beach. It took all of three minutes. This was what made it all worthwhile, I figured when I stretched out on the sand. All this sun and beach and Pacific Ocean, and why the hell was I getting nostalgic for the sight of the Central Park lake the whole time?

I was ready and waiting for Melanie Rigby when seven-thirty came around. She was punctual, still wearing the same blue shirt and blue jeans, and carrying an impressive-looking attaché case. We went down to the sidewalk and I discovered she was driving one of those dinky little Japanese cars that look like they should have a big wind-up key sticking out of the trunk.

"It gets me around just fine," the big blonde said in a defensive voice, "and the mileage is real great."

She drove down the main drag, out on the coastal road that sweeps past Sublime Point, and then made a right turn. The new road took us past the almost finished development of manmade canals with a large motel in the center, strategically surrounded by cabanas. Then the road started the long climb into the hills.

"He's rich?" I said.

"Who?"

"Broderick. Your husband, remember?"

"Oh, sure," she said. "He's rich. His daddy was rich before him. Broderick comes from a very rich family."

"What does he do?"

"He owns some hunks of real estate in and around Santo Bahia," she said. "He's got a big piece of that motel and canal complex we passed a few miles back, for example."

We made a left turn onto a narrower road, and the overhang of trees on either side of the road made the sky suddenly darker. After a couple of minutes she switched on the headlights, and they cut a steady swath through the gathering gloom ahead of us.

"We've been married for almost three years," Melanie Rigby said. "We might almost have made it, if it hadn't been for his goddamned bitch of a sister."

"She got in the way?"

"She was never out of the way. She lived with us the whole time. Some nights, there, I almost expected to find her in bed with us." Her voice was bitter. "You couldn't know what it was like, Danny. Living in the same house with somebody who disapproved of everything you said, and did!"

"Why didn't you move out?"

"I wanted to, but Broderick refused. He refused to toss out Sarah, too. It was like she had some hold over him and he was scared of her. Maybe they had a cosy incestuous relationship before we were married, and maybe they still had one after we were married. I don't know, and I don't goddamned care."

"How much do you figure on taking him for in the divorce settlement?" I asked.

"I got me a good lawyer from out of town," she told me. "No lawyer in Santo Bahia wanted to know from it. They're all into Broderick for something."

"You didn't answer my question."

"If you want to make it a nice round figure, you could say a half million," she said. "I'm going for the

6

big one. It will squeeze Broderick for sure, but it's not about to break him. And after I collect, I'm off like the breeze. To hell and gone out of this fucking resort!"

"Only he's still arguing about the settlement," I said. "Is that why you're seeing him tonight?"

"He's been arguing ever since the beginning, right after the moment he stopped screaming," she said contemptuously. "But tonight is different, he says. He's suddenly all sweetness and light, and it makes me feel nervous."

There was a fork in the road ahead and we veered left. A few seconds later Melanie slowed the car as it bumped its way along an unpaved track that climbed steeply, twisting as it climbed.

"It's not far now," she said. "Maybe another half mile."

"A half-mile to a half million," I said. "How does little sister like the idea?"

"Her insides are knotted out of shape, I bet!" she snorted. "She figures the Rigby clan has a kind of divine right to keep all their ill-gotten loot."

The car made another abrupt turn, bumped along an even narrower track for a couple of hundred yards, then came to a stop. Caught in the headlights' beam, the two-story facade of the house in front of us looked enormous.

"The little log cabin?" I muttered.

"Broderick likes to entertain here a lot," Melanie said casually. "My guess is he originally had it designed for lots of lovely orgies, but little sister never approved. The first floor is one big living room, with a kitchen at the back. There are six bedrooms and a couple of bathrooms on the second floor. The whole goddamned place is wood-paneled. He even

7

had the chandeliers made from old coach wheels and suspended by iron chains. But they weighed around three hundred pounds each, so he had to have the ceiling reinforced. We spent our honeymoon here, would you believe? I guess the nearest Broderick ever got to having an orgy, was having me on a fur rug, with all the chandeliers blazing with light. It was like being the star in some goddamned porn movie!"

She cut the motor and switched off the headlights. The sudden and complete darkness was unnerving.

"I forgot to bring a flashlight," she said, "but I guess we can grope our way into the house."

"Maybe we can grope our way into an orgy on the fur rug, without bothering with the blazing chandeliers," I suggested.

"And have Broderick walk in on us when we're about five seconds away from a big climax?" She snorted derisively. "You're just the good and trusted friend come to see nothing violent happens between me and Broderick, Boyd, and don't you forget it."

We got out of the car and walked slowly toward the house. Melanie had been there before and that was why she knew there were three steps leading up onto the front porch, I figured, the moment after I had tripped and rapped my shinbone painfully against the edge of the first step. Then I joined her on the top step while she fumbled in her purse for the keys, then fumbled with them again until she found the keyhole. The front door opened and the inside of the house looked even blacker than the world outside. It was only a question of degree, but I wouldn't have believed it possible. Melanie walked inside confidently and there was a sharp click a couple of seconds later.

"Hell!" she said. "The lights aren't working."

8

"We could have an orgy in the dark," I said. "That way, Broderick won't be able to see us even if he does walk in when we're just five seconds away from a big climax."

"Maybe it's just one circuit gone," she said. "I'll try one of the table lamps."

A small flame appeared from between her fingers, and I realized she was holding a cigarette lighter.

"You wait here," she said.

"I'll wait here," I agreed, and took time out to rub my shin.

The flickering light moved farther into the room, and then I heard another click.

"The table lamp isn't working, either," she said. "Maybe—*ugh!*"

"Ugh?"

"Something wet just hit me," she said. "It would be just like that moron to have left the bath running the last time he was here!"

"Maybe he switched off the power the last time he was here," I suggested.

"Maybe he did," she said. "*Ugh!* There's another one."

"So where's the fuse box?"

"Around the back of the house someplace."

The flickering light headed back toward me, then went out.

"You'd better take this," she said, and thrust the lighter into my hand. "I'll wait here."

"If I never come back," I said, "you can use my two hundred dollars to erect a statue someplace on Sublime Point in everloving memory."

"It'll have to be something small for that kind of money," she said. "Something about eight inches long and a two-inch circumference would be flattering, right? But it would be a permament erection, of course."

The night wasn't quite so completely black now as I fumbled my way around the side of the house toward the back. My eyes were beginning to get used to the darkness finally, because the bulk of the house now seemed slightly darker than the rest of the night. I got around to the back of the house and flicked Melanie's lighter into flame. It wasn't any big problem to resolve. The black box held all the fuses, and somebody had pulled the master switch. With all the confidence born out of my innate technical skill, I switched it on again. Then the whole goddamned house lighted up like some gigantic neon sign. From someplace inside the house Melanie screamed, and kept right on screaming.

I raced around to the front of the house and into the huge living room. Melanie was just standing there, her eyes tight-shut, still screaming her fool head off. The front of her blue silk shirt had a couple of large wet stains, I noticed—kind of a red brown-color. While I was standing there gaping at her there was a faint splashing sound, and a blob of red-brown liquid spattered on the floor at Melanie's feet. I looked up instinctively, then wished I hadn't bothered. Like Melanie had told me, the chandeliers were made from old coach wheels, hung from the ceiling by heavy iron chains. But the one almost directly above her head had only a couple of lightbulbs still working. The rest were obscured by the bulk of the body that lay across the coach wheel, tilting it sharply to one side. He was a big guy and he lay face-downward, his eyes wide open and not staring at anything in particular. As I looked, another large globule of blood dripped from his ripped-out throat

and spattered onto the floor. Melanie stopped screaming and the silence was almost unbearable. Then she
opened her eyes and stared at me.

"Broderick?" I mumbled.

"Broderick!" she said thickly.

Her eyes rolled up into her head and I just missed
catching her as she passed out cold.

Chapter Two

~~~~~~

She wasn't wearing a bra, but it was a warm night so I figured she wouldn't catch cold. I had washed her shirt clean of the bloodstains and now it was tumbling around in the drier. I had also grabbed a bottle of brandy from the bar, and we sat in the kitchen drinking it while we waited for Melanie's shirt to dry out, and a little inspiration. She took a large swallow of brandy, shivered, then wrapped her arms tight around her beautiful breasts.

"Oh, God!" she said. "It was like a nightmare when the lights suddenly came on. I saw those stains on my shirt, then I looked up, and there he was staring down at me with his throat—"

"Sure," I said quickly. "Try not to think about it."

"It was nice of you to bring me in here, Danny," she said, "so I didn't have to see him again when I woke up. If I had, I think I would have gone clean out of my mind!"

"Practical," I said, "that's me. Somebody had a good idea, putting a washer and drier in the kitchen."

"Me," she said. "There just isn't any laundry around here. In fact, there's nothing around here except this house for miles and—Danny!—what are we going to do?"

"Get out of here when your shirt is dry enough to put back on," I said. "We should also call the police."

"There isn't any phone here," she said. "Broderick would never have one put in. It would destroy his privacy, he said."

"Somebody destroyed more than his privacy," I said. "How did he get here in the first place?"

"He—" she stared at me again—"oh, I see what you mean. No car."

"It's too far to walk," I said. "Somebody gave him a lift, maybe?"

"Then killed him? Who would do a thing like that?"

"His little sister?"

"Sarah?" She shook her head. "I don't know. I don't even want to think about it right now."

"I wish there was a phone right here," I said.

"So you could call the police?"

"Something like that," I said. "It would look a hell of a lot better for the both of us."

Her face got that gray look about it again. "You're trying to tell me something, Danny, and I don't think I want to know."

"I know one of the local cops," I said, and my insides cringed as I remembered. "Captain Schnell. He's like most other cops, he won't want to believe in a phantom killer."

"I knew I wasn't going to like it," she said.

"His first premise will be you hired me to kill your husband," I said moodily. "His second premise will be we drove him up here, then I killed him."

"What with?" Melanie said quickly. "I mean, you don't have a knife with you, right?"

"Whoever killed him would have wiped off any fingerprints," I said. "Then, who knows what they did with the murder weapon? Maybe they just tossed it into the bushes. For sure, they would have left it someplace where it'll be real easy for the police to find."

"I knew I didn't want to hear this," she said miserably, "but there's still more to come, right?"

"Whoever killed him must have known he had a date to meet you here," I said. "So they killed him not long before we arrived. Then they drove away again, knowing you'd probably find the body and then what?"

"Go to pieces the way I did." She smiled wanly.

"I think maybe we should get the hell out of here," I said.

I stopped the drier and took out her shirt. It was still damp, but pneumonia was the least of her worries right then, I figured.

"Here." I tossed the shirt to her. "Put that on."

"It's still damp."

"Into each life, a little damp must fall," I said. "Put it on and let's get out of here!"

She put the shirt on, shivered again, then drank the rest of her brandy. I washed and dried both glasses, then returned them and the bottle to the bar. Then I grabbed hold of her elbow and steered her back through the living room toward the front door. She kept her eyes carefully downcast all the time and I didn't blame her one little bit. We got out onto the front porch and I closed the door in back of me, then told her to wait in the car. I went around to the back of the house and pulled the master switch inside the fuse box. The sudden total blackness didn't help any, but I managed to stumble my way back to the car.

"What are we going to do now, Danny?" she asked in a small voice.

"Is there another way down to the coast?" I asked her. "A different route from the way we came?"

"Sure," she said. "It's longer."

"Let's take it," I said.

She started the motor, switched on the headlights, then made a tight U-turn.

"The only thing the killer didn't know was you'd asked me along for the ride," I said. "So he would have figured you'd arrive, go inside the house, find the body, and—like you just said—fall apart. So maybe he had the cute idea of making an anonymous call to the cops and telling them they'll find a body in the house."

"Oh, God!" Melanie said. "And they'd find me there with those bloodstains on my shirt and—"

"Right," I said. "So where have we been tonight?"

The car hit a vicious bump in the road that flattened the springs. Melanie made a thin cawing sound deep in her throat, then pushed harder on the gaspedal.

"You mean we're not going to call the police?" she said around ten seconds later.

"You're damned right we're not," I said. "We're going to set up some kind of an alibi for tonight. Where are you living?"

"I'm renting one of those goddamned tourist cottages on Paradise Beach," she said. "Why?"

"Who else knows about your date to meet Broderick at the log cabin tonight?"

"I don't know," she said. "I didn't tell anybody else about it—except you, of course."

"But you don't know who Broderick told?" I said. "He told the murderer, for sure."

15

"I wish you wouldn't keep on reminding me," she muttered.

"Okay," I said. "So you can tell the first part of the story straight. You were nervous when he asked you to meet him at the cabin, so you hired me to go with you. But I persuaded you not to go. Too dangerous, I said. And, in parentheses, I was right. With hindsight I'm always brilliant. So I figured when you didn't show, Broderick would come looking for you, and it could be safer for you if I kept you company. So you invited me over to your cottage on Paradise Beach."

"Okay," she said. "But are you sure this is all necessary, Danny? I mean, why don't we just tell them the truth?"

"I figured I'd been all through that," I said patiently. "Little sister, Broderick's lawyers, and maybe half the population of Santo Bahia know you were both arguing about the size of the settlement. Were you his first wife?"

"Yes," she said.

"No children?"

"No children."

"Even if he altered his will when you broke up, you'll still have one hell of a claim against his estate. Even half would be a hell of a lot more than five hundred thousand dollars, right?"

"Oh, God!" she said again. "Now I'm beginning to see what you mean."

"Whoever killed him had you in mind as the patsy," I said. "They won't give up easy."

She shivered again. "Danny, you've got to help me!"

"That's what I figure I'm doing right now," I said sourly.

"I'm sorry!"

"Don't be sorry, be real careful," I said.

She was right about one thing. The alternate route back to the coast road made the return journey around fifteen miles longer than the original run to the log cabin. It was around a quarter of eleven when we arrived at Paradise Beach, and most of the beach cottages were lighted up like Christmas trees. There was the rich scent of magnolia blossom and twelve-year-old Scotch heavy in the air. Melanie parked the car out front of the very last beach cottage, and we got out. I followed her inside and she switched on the lights as we went. She homed in on the bar and set up a couple of tall glasses.

"Always stay with the same drink, until the drink leaves you," she said. "Old Melanie proverb."

"Brandy will do just fine for me, too," I said. "On the rocks."

"Fine old Napoleon brandy," she said in a horrified voice. "On the rocks?"

"I'll make the drinks," I told her. "Your shirt must still be damp, the way it's clinging to—well—damp!"

"Who cares?" she said. "You're not thinking of turning into a sex maniac at a time like this, right?"

"We've been here for the last three hours supposedly waiting for your husband to show, after you never kept the date with him at the cabin, remember?" I said. "And you're wearing a damp shirt?"

She chewed on her lower lip for a moment. "I'm sorry, Danny. I guess I'm not thinking too straight right now."

I watched her walk out of the room, then went across to the bar and made the drinks. If the killer had tipped off the cops and they had found the body already, it wouldn't take them long to finger Melanie Rigby, I figured. So the thing was to get into a

17

relaxed frame of mind, and I took a swift gulp of brandy to help. Then the doorbell rang, and I slopped fine Napoleon brandy across the bartop.

"Danny?" Melanie's voice was at least an octave too high.

"Take it easy," I called back. "I'll get it."

Another mouthful of brandy helped. I took a deep breath and put what I hoped was a nonchalant look onto my face, then walked toward the door. The doorbell rang again the moment before I opened the front door. There were three of them—two men and a woman. A brunette, with her sleek lustrous hair brushed smoothly against the sides of her head from a center-part. Her dark eyes held a steady unblinking gaze, and her fine-chiseled features gave her an aristocratic look. She was wearing a white pantsuit that fit her athletic-looking figure real close, emphasizing the high thrust of her small breasts, and the length of her elegant tapering legs. Her mouth, I idly noticed, was sensual without being vulnerable. Most of the female Borgias would have looked like that, I guessed.

"Well," she said in a deep contralto, "what have we here? The corespondent?"

"And who the hell are you?" I asked elegantly.

She started walking. We either would have a head-on collision, or I moved to one side. So I moved to one side. She swept on past me into the living room, and the two guys followed her. She came to a stop in the center of the living room and looked around her like she was slumming, and not liking it too well.

"All right," she said. "Where is she?"

"Who?"

"Melanie. Who the hell else?" she said tightly. "And who the hell are you?"

"I asked first, remember?" I said.

18

"I'm her dear sister-in-law," she said. "Sarah Rigby."

"I'm Danny Boyd," I said. "Melanie's powdering her nose, or something, right now."

"I'm sure it needs it," she said. "Her nose, or whatever it is she's powdering. Charles, I'll have a drink. My usual."

"Sure."

The guy who moved across to the bar was somewhere in his early forties, I figured. Neat black hair with a touch of gray at the temples, a deep tan, and an athletic stride. Real rich background, the right kind of degree from the right kind of university, and now working in a profession. Law, I figured sourly, would be about right for him.

"This is Charles Gray," Sarah Rigby declared. "My attorney. He also happens to be a close personal friend of mine."

"Hi," I said.

"Good evening, Mr. Boyd." Gray started making drinks with great concentration.

"And this is Bobo Shanks," the brunette said. "Another good friend of mine."

Shanks was maybe ten years younger than Gray. A big guy, and he looked to be mostly muscle. He had long blond hair, a matching mustache, and bright blue eyes. He looked so goddamned ingenuous it couldn't true.

"Hi." He grinned at me, showing pearly-white teeth. "I know it sounds gruesome, but you get tagged with a diminutive when you're a kid and you're stuck with it for the rest of your life!"

Melanie came back into the room, having substituted a pink silk shirt for the blue. Makeup had put

19

some color back onto her face but she still didn't look good.

."What the hell are you doing here?" she asked stonily.

"Just checking," the brunette said. "I was curious to know how the meeting went with my dear brother this evening."

"I didn't go," Melanie said. "Danny advised me not to, so I didn't. Is that my drink?"

"Sure," I said.

It was beginning to sound like the one word was going to be my total contribution to the evening. I walked across to the bar and picked up the drinks I had made, then gave one to Melanie. She took it with her across to the couch and sat down.

"You didn't go?" Sarah Rigby said in an incredulous voice.

"I just told you," Melanie snapped.

"You mean you let Broderick go all the way up to the cabin for nothing?"

"I'm glad I'm finally getting through to you," Melanie said.

"On Dannys' advice?" the brunette repeated. Her dark eyes stared at me with open hostility. "And who the hell are you to give advice, Boyd? Some two-bit lawyer?"

"I'm a private detective," I said. "Mrs. Rigby consulted me this afternoon and, like she just told you, I advised her not to keep the appointment."

"A private detective?" The way she said it, pimping would have been a respectable occupation by comparison.

"They're about to be divorced," I said. "Suddenly her husband wants to discuss the settlement secretly in a place to hell and gone in the hills someplace. Who knows what he had in mind, exactly."

"A tiny answer," she said, "from a tiny mind!"

"It's not unreasonable advice," Gray said. "From an outsider, I mean."

"Who the fuck asked you to comment?" the brunette said tartly.

A pinched look showed up on Gray's face, then he gave a slight shrug.

"I'm only your attorney," he said in a mild voice.

"Sorry, Charles." She took the drink out of his hand and sipped it slowly. "It's just that I would have thought Melanie was a Rigby for long enough to know better. Than to hire some tawdry peephole-artist, I mean."

"So now you know, and there's nothing more to entertain you, Miss Rigby," I said briskly. "But finish your drinks before you leave, by all means. They're two dollars each, and if you care to leave a gratuity, I'll be real grateful."

"I'm in no hurry," she said tightly. "You'll have to contain your lust for a while longer, Boyd. But don't worry. Melanie always was a pushover for anything in pants old enough to get it up!"

"It was like that the whole time we were married," Melanie said. "If you opened a container of orange juice in the morning, guess who popped out?"

"I remember, not long after they were married, somebody asked me to define a nymphomaniac," Sarah Rigby said flatly. "As I recall, I said any woman who liked sex only half as much as Melanie does."

"I guess if Melanie never saw Broderick tonight, there's not much point in our staying any longer," Shanks said in a slightly hesitant voice.

"We've only got her word for it," Sarah said silkily.

"What the hell is that supposed to mean?" Melanie said, and her voice had jumped that whole god-damned octave again.

"I mean, maybe you did see Broderick tonight," Sarah said. "And you took your strongarm along with you." One lean finger pointed contemptuously at me. "For all we know, poor Broderick could be still up at the cabin, lying on the floor after being brutally beaten by Boyd here." She paused for a moment. "Or worse, even!"

"Don't let your imagination run riot, Sarah," Gray said. "The chances are Broderick got tired of waiting and is probably home now, and waiting for us."

"Very well." The brunette put her unfinished drink back onto the bartop. "There's one easy way to find out. But if he isn't waiting for us at home, I'm going to drive up to the cabin and find out what's happened to him."

"Broderick's old enough to take care of himself," Gray said easily. "If he's not home, he could be any place. The club, for example?"

"I know your fine legal mind needs all the rest it can get," Sarah said. "But Bobo will drive me up there if necessary, won't you, Bobo?"

Shanks grinned easily. "Sure, my pleasure."

"So that's settled," she said determinedly. "You can bill me for the drinks, Boyd!"

She swept out of the room with her nose tilted in the air, like the duchess who made the unfortunate mistake of getting downwind of the peasants. Bobo grinned amiably at nobody special, then followed her out of the room.

"You have to make allowances for Sarah," Gray

muttered as he headed toward the door. "She's very fond of her brother."

"There's a word for it," I said brightly. "But, you being a lawyer, I guess you'd know it already."

He stopped for a moment in the doorway and looked back at me. "You want to watch that mouth of yours, Boyd," he said coldly. "Or somebody may ram a fist down it."

The front door closed in back of them, and we heard the car start up a couple of seconds later.

"Danny!" Melanie wailed. "What the hell are we going to do now?"

It was getting to be a refrain.

Chapter Three

"Maybe she won't go up to the cabin," I said.

"She'll go," Melanie said listlessly. "I know that bitch!"

"Gray's her attorney," I said. "How about Shanks?"

"I never did know about him," Melanie said. "Except that I never liked him. The old faithful family friend, with that idiot grin plastered all over his face the whole time. I guess if anybody's ever broken the seal it's him."

"The seal?" I queried.

"The one with the family crest stamped on it," she said. "The one that Sarah wears like a big no-entry sign!"

"It wasn't that big a secret," I said. "Broderick told little sister about it, right?"

"And she brought the hired help and old buddy Bobo along with her," Melanie said. "Why, Danny?"

"You mean, why not wait and find out what happened from Broderick?"

"Right," she said. "Why?"

"It's a good question," I allowed. "I'll try and think up an answer for you." I checked my watch and found it was half past eleven. "I figure I should go now."

"You can't leave me now!" she wailed. "I'll go out of my mind all alone with nothing to think about but that chandelier and Broderick just lying there looking down at me, with his throat—"

"I have to go," I said. "The three of them visited and established we were here together. So that's okay. I'm just your hired help, remember? You'd reasonably figure if Broderick went to the cabin and you didn't show, he wouldn't have waited more than an hour, at most. So, if he was going to visit with you on his way home, he would have done it by now. Consequently, there's no logical reason to keep the hired help here any longer."

"*Danny!*"

The drink dropped out of her hand as she jumped up from the couch. Then her body cannoned into mind, and her arms wrapped tight around my neck. I could feel the yielding warmth of her full breasts squashed against my chest, and my arms went around her automatically.

"You can't go!" she breathed into my ear. "I'll go crazy here all by myself. My nerve ends are screaming already. Sex is the only thing that's going to keep me sane, Danny!"

"How will it look if the police walk in on us?" I said. "The wife and her lover making love, having just murdered her husband."

Her arms wrapped even tighter around my neck. Her thighs pressed against mine, her pelvis bumped into mine, and despite myself, things began to stir. "I don't care!" she said thickly. "You have to understand me, Danny! If I don't have you right now, I'll wind up walking up the wall!" Her pelvis screwed more

25

tightly into mine. Her hands fluttered down my back to my buttocks. She pulled them hard against her. I could feel the small yielding area between her legs against my crotch.

"Okay," I said huskily.

"Thank you," she said softly. "You won't regret it, Danny, I promise."

"Why don't you go into the bedroom and get ready?" I said. "I'll finish my drink in here while I'm waiting."

She pulled her head back and looked at me suspiciously. "You won't run out on me?"

"I promise," I said. "Us Boyds never break a promise. Not where sex is concerned, anyway."

"I won't be long."

She was almost running by the time she reached the door. I picked up my drink and finished it in three quick gulps. Another half gallon of brandy might have helped, but I doubted it right then. Melanie Rigby must have been the fastest undresser of all time.

"I'm ready, Danny," her breathless voice called out a few seconds later.

I put the empty glass back onto the bartop and walked toward the bedroom. The door was wide open, and the only light came from a heavily-shaded lamp beside the bed. Melanie lay on the bed, her head cradled in her hands, and her legs wide apart. Her naked body had a rich, soft sheen to it in the soft light from the table lamp—the coral-colored nipples lifting in tumescence, the soft deep curve of her belly, and the tangled bush of blond hair that ranged down the gentle slopes between her legs. I felt a definite physical change as I looked at her, and knew I had to be out of my mind. But when my shaft is on the scent of easy conquest, it's hell's own job to try and make it see reason. I could see it would be a struggle.

"Danny," she said as I walked across to the bed. "Aren't you getting undressed first?"

"Sure," I said. "But I need a kiss to keep me going that long, okay?"

"Okay!" She laughed as she sat up.

"So close your eyes and pucker up," I told her.

"You keep on talking this way and I'll think I'm back in junior high," she said.

"How can I kiss you if you never stop talking?" I asked plaintively.

She lifted her head obediently and closed her eyes. I measured the distance carefully, then clipped her on the point of the jaw. Her eyes glazed, then she fell back on the bed and just lay there. The rigidity went out of my disbelieving shaft as I rolled her under the covers and smoothed back her hair from her face. She had left the car keys on the dash, I remembered gratefully, and since there was no way she would need the car for the rest of the night, I felt sure she wouldn't mind if I borrowed it. I switched off the table lamp, then went back to the living room and tidied up the glasses, thinking it was the least I could do. Then I opened the front door and was about to switch off the last remaining light when a figure suddenly loomed up on the front porch.

"Boyd," a bleak voice said, "it figures!"

"Captain Schell," I said, and automatically took a step backward. "It figures?"

"How long back was it that you hung our your dirty little shingle in Santo Bahia?" he said. "A week, at most, right? And what do I get now? A body, that's what, Boyd. Like I said, it figures!"

"A body?" I said brightly. "What body?"

"Let's go inside," he said. "I want to talk with the lady of the house. *And* you!"

I backed into the living room, switching lights on again as I went. Schell stopped just inside the door and his hooded eyes under the close-cropped gray hair looked at me with immense distaste, like I was the contents of some cadaver's stomach the crime lab had produced for his special scrutiny.

"Okay," he said. "Where have you been all night, Boyd?"

"Here," I said, "with Mrs. Rigby."

"I guess this is going to take a long time," he said. "I'll have a drink. Scotch, with soda."

He went over to the couch and sat down with his legs sprawled out in front of him. I made the drink, gave it to him, then made one for myself.

"Just you and Mrs. Rigby," he said finally. "All by yourselves?"

"Up until around a half hour back," I said. "Then we had visitors."

"Who?"

"Her sister-in-law, Sarah Rigby, an attorney called Gray, and some guy who said his name was Bobo Shanks."

"Bobo Shanks?" Schell said. "Jesus!"

"And that's about it," I said hopefully.

"Old friends?" he said. "You just happened to stop by for a visit?"

"She's a client of mine," I said. "In the middle of a divorce. Her husband wanted her to meet him secretly in a log cabin way up in the hills. She got scared, so she came to me. I advised her not to go. Any settlement can be figured out between their attorneys, I told her."

"So then she was so grateful she invited you home for the evening."

"She was scared how her husband would react after she had stood him up," I said. "She figured he could come calling and be violent. So she wanted me around just in case, to cool him off."

"Where is she now?"

"In bed," I said. "She was tired, and was feeling a hell of a lot of nervous strain with it, I guess. So she took some tranquilizers and went to bed. I was just leaving when you walked up onto the front porch. What the hell is this all about, Captain?"

"I thought you'd never ask!" He sipped his drink, and his face brightened momentarily. "This isn't bad Scotch."

"You said something about a body?"

"That's right. I'm glad you remembered. Somebody called in and told us about that cabin in the hills. He was out hunting, the guy said."

"Hunting what?"

"He didn't say." Schell shrugged gently. "But he heard these screams coming from the cabin. When he got close he saw a man and a woman rush out of the house, get into a car, and drive away. The descriptions he gave us fit you and the Rigby woman real good. You, anyway. I'll find out about the Rigby woman when I see her in a couple of minutes. The guy took a look inside the cabin and saw a body swinging on the chandelier, he said. So he figured we should go take a look, but he didn't give us his name because he didn't want to get involved."

"And you took a look?" I prompted.

"Broderick Rigby," he said. "That was the body's name. And swinging on the chandelier like the guy said, with his throat cut from ear to ear. A real mess!"

29

"How the hell did he get up onto the chandelier?" I said.

"What the hell kind of stupid goddamned question is that?" he growled. "We found the murder weapon in a bush a couple of yards from the front door. A breadknife. With a serrated edge, yet! It means whoever killed him literally sawed away at his throat until—"

"You don't need to be so graphic," I told him. "I get the complete picture."

"I figure he was either unconscious, or somebody held him while somebody else hacked away at his throat," he said. "What did Miss Rigby want?"

"She wanted to know the result of the meeting between Mrs. Rigby and her husband," I said. "She seemed real disappointed when Mrs. Rigby told her she never kept the appointment."

"No other visitors?" he asked. "Like between eight-thirty and nine-thirty, say?"

"No other visitors."

"You want to wake up Mrs. Rigby, or should I do it?"

"It's not going to be easy," I said. "I don't know just how many pills she took, exactly, but—"

I could have saved my breath. "*Danny!*" a hysterical voice screamed, and the next moment Melanie came running into the room. Stark naked, her full breasts bouncing wildly, and her hair streaming every which way. Like she had suddenly missed me at the seven-day orgy, and I had been the best lay she'd found in the first four days.

"Danny!" she sobbed. "You hit me! You hit me and then you sneaked out on me. I told you sex is the only thing that'll stop me from walking up the wall. Every time I remember his face staring down at me from the chandelier I—"

"Melanie," I said, and cleared my throat gently. "I don't think you've met Captain Schell."

"Captain Schell?" She looked at me wildly, and then her whole body started to shake uncontrollably. The effect was totally erotic, and that didn't help any, either. "Captain Schell," she repeated in a quavering voice. "A *police* captain!"

"Why don't you go put some clothes on, Mrs. Rigby," Schell said in a gentle voice. "Then come back here and tell me that bit again about how every time you remember his face staring down at you from the chandelier, and like that?"

She turned around slowly, took one hesitant step back toward the bedroom, and then her knees buckled under her and she hit the floor with a solid thump.

"Maybe if I put her back to bed?" I said. "I figure she's had enough for one night. I can tell you the story, okay?"

"I can't wait to hear it," Schell said. "Maybe I'll help myself to another Scotch while you're taking care of the lady." His eyes widened for a moment. "All she wanted from you was sex, and you slugged her?"

"It just hasn't been my night," I admitted.

I picked up Melanie awkwardly and carried her back into the bedroom, then put her back onto the bed. If she had any goddamned sense, I thought bitterly, the next time she woke up she'd stay right where she was and bury her head under the pillows. Schell was busy helping himself to another Scotch when I got back into the living room. I took a quick gulp of my own drink, then told him the true story.

31

He went back to the couch and sat down again while I was still talking, the glass cradled in his hands. There was a kind of dull silence after I had finished, which lasted around five agonizing seconds.

"You don't expect me to believe it?" he said finally.

"No," I said, "that's why I lied the first time around."

"Second time around," he said. "You lied to Miss Rigby and her companions."

"That's why I lied both times around," I agreed. "I wouldn't believe it myself."

"Rigby was over six feet tall and would have weighed around 180 pounds," he said. "The chandelier is at least nine feet off the floor. Why the hell bother to put him up there?"

"Hope he wouldn't be seen?" I suggested. "Whoever killed him figured Melanie would wait around for a while, and the longer she waited the greater chance of you finding her still there."

"Don't be more stupid than you look, Boyd," he said in a tired voice. "Blood was still dripping from his throat onto the floor when we got there."

"You're right," I said. "Some of it dripped onto Melanie's shirt, and when she found out what it was she nearly went out of her mind."

"She only had to look up to see where it was coming from," he said.

"The place was in darkness when we arrived," I told him. "She walked in first and tried the light switches and nothing happened. I went around to the back and found the fuse box. Somebody had pulled the master switch. So she was all alone in the house when the lights came on, and then she saw him up on the chandelier."

He drank some of his Scotch. "They were in the

middle of the divorce and arguing about the settlement. Then he asked her to meet him up at the log
cabin and she got nervous and asked you to go along
with her, right?"

"Right," I said, "and he told his little sister about
the meeting, too."

"And she told the attorney and Bobo Shanks!"
Schell almost grunted. "Okay, with any luck she told
a hundred other people, so I have loads of suspects."

"He was dead when we got there," I said. "I don't
expect you to believe it, but—"

"Why?" he interrupted.

"Why, what?"

"Why don't you expect me to believe your story?"

"Because—" I stopped, and stared at him. "You believe it?"

"Not all of it," he said. "I know you, Boyd. You're a
devious son of a bitch, and I'll bet there's something
vital you left out. But we'll get around to it later. I
know you'd steal your poor old grannie's glasses so
she couldn't see you taking her life savings out from
under the mattress, but I don't see you committing
cold-blooded murder. And from what I've seen of
Mrs. Rigby—and that's about the only real interesting
thing I have seen tonight—I don't see her sawing
away at her husband's throat while you held his arms,
either. That's all I'm prepared to say right now."

"Right now I figured you'd be booking the both of
us on a murder charge," I said.

"Don't let it go to your head!" He finished his
drink, then got up onto his feet. "And don't do anything obviously stupid like trying to leave town,
right? And keep your goddamned pointed nose out of
this thing, Boyd. Broderick Rigby was a big deal
around Santo Bahia, and this is going to make waves.

I don't want to be tripping over you every time I turn around." He tossed his empty glass at me and I caught it awkwardly. "The both of you can come down in the morning—sometime around eleven—and make statements."

He started walking toward the door and I stared blankly at his back.

"Thanks," I said, and almost choked on a word I never thought I would use to Schell, "Captain."

"Don't thank me yet," he said, over his shoulder. "Come morning and I could have changed my mind."

I heard the front door slam in back of him, then picked up my drink and drained the glass in one long swallow.

"*Danny!*" a frantic voice called from the bedroom.

"I know," I called back. "What do we do now?"

The hell with it! I thought suddenly, because I knew exactly what we did now. I headed toward the bedroom, shedding clothes as I went. By the time I walked into the bedroom I was wearing nothing at all.

"Danny?" Melanie was sitting bolt upright in bed, her eyes wide with fear. The blankets had fallen away from the upper part of her body, and her nipples stared at me like frozen exclamation marks. "Are we under arrest?"

"You're not going to believe this," I said, "but Schell accepts our story. The true story."

"You're not just trying to make things easier for me?" she pleaded.

"I'm trying to make things hard for you right now," I said. "Or the singular, to be accurate. But you're not making it easy for me to make it hard and—the hell with it!—don't you want to relax and be able to go to sleep."

"How can I?" she wailed.

"I plan to demonstrate," I said.

I switched off the table lamp and got into bed beside her. Her arms wound tight around my neck and her body pressed firmly against mine. Alerted, my shaft leaped to attention and prodded her soft belly with an interrogative gesture.

"Danny," she whispered. "Is it really all right?"

"Everything is just fine," I said. "All you have to do now is relax."

I slid my hands down her back until they cupped the well-rounded cheeks of her bottom, and squeezed them hard. She made a soft sound of assent, and her mouth closed hungrily against mine. And then all four hands got busy in a gentle exploration. One of my hands found her left breast and teased the erect nipple, while the other one slid between her legs and made a lingering exploration of the moist intimate warmth that nestled there. My fingers slowly moistened as they quested in between her labial lips, gently opening her up to receive me. While they were doing this, her own hand was caressing my rampant stalk, so skillfully that I had to stop her before a premature ejaculation deposited my burning seed all over the palm of her hand—a disaster that would have done no one any credit, least of all one Danny Boyd, the last of the Latin lovers. So, taking the initiative, my body poised over hers, I eased her legs apart and with a couple of quick thrusts, brought myself into her. She moaned softly, and then her body began to move with mine in delicious harmony, our movements becoming wilder, more frenetic as, coupled in a rare combination of passion and gentleness, we reached toward a prolonged, tumultuous climax. Afterward, she murmured sweet words of content, then went to sleep in my arms. It took me a while to get to sleep. The only thing I could see in my mind's eye was the body slumped across the chandelier, the unseeing eyes staring downward, and the gaping throat with the blood still dripping from it in a slow, measured beat.

Chapter Four

~~~~~~

We made our statements the next morning and signed them. Then Schell took us to the morgue and Melanie identified the body as that of her late husband, Broderick Rigby. The morgue attendant was delicate enough to pull the sheet back only as far as the chin. The color drained out of Melanie's face, then she nodded stiffly.

"It's him," she whispered.

"Thank you, Mrs. Rigby," Schell said. "His sister has also identified the body, about a half hour back."

"Sarah knows about it?" Melanie said numbly. "How goddamned stupid of me. Of course, she has to know."

"How did you know it was Rigby last night?" I asked Schell.

"I recognized him," Schell said flatly. "He was a well-known figure around here. Met him a couple of times at civic functions."

"You know any more than you did last night?" I said.

"Not much," he said. "The autopsy will be sometime early this afternoon." He made a production out

37

of checking his watch. "I should be someplace else already," he said. "Thank you, Mrs. Rigby."

He started walking quickly, and by the time we were outside the morgue, Schell had disappeared. We climbed back into Melanie's car, but she made no effort to start the motor.

"Sarah will be sure I killed him," she said in a monotone. "I'm scared, Danny."

"Of her?"

She nodded quickly. "You don't know her the way I do. I don't want to go back to the cottage, Danny. Not yet, anyway."

"So where would you like to go?" I asked politely.

"There's a restaurant out on a bay about fifteen miles down the coast. Why don't we go there for lunch?"

"Okay," I said.

"You can put the tab on my tab." She smiled wanly. "I still owe you two hundred dollars."

"Okay," I said gallantly.

She started the motor. "Last night you said I'll probably get more money now that Broderick's dead than I would have from the settlement, right?"

"Right," I agreed.

"But if I'm found guilty of his murder I won't get a dime. Never mind what else will happen to me."

"Right again," I said.

"Sarah will try to prove it was me who killed him," she said. "My God! Will she ever try! I want you to fine the murderer, Danny, and I don't care how much it costs."

"I'll be happy to have you as a client, Melanie," I said. "So put a price tag on it."

"What?" She looked at me in surprise.

"Right now you probably figure a hundred thousand dollars is reasonable," I said, "but afterward you could just as easily figure five thousand dollars was exorbitant. So now is the time to put a price tag on it."

"You're a hard man, Danny," she said.

"I figure I proved that last night, already," I said.

"And a vulgar one, too." She smiled briefly. "You put a price on it."

"A thousand for expenses, and you don't see that again whatever happens," I said promptly. "Another five thousand if I find the killer."

"It sounds reasonable," she said. "You have yourself a deal, Danny."

But she didn't sound all that happy about it. Maybe she figured I should have had a more romantic approach. She should have realized an heiress in distress is a hell of a lot different from a damsel with the same problem. Damsels don't get to hire private detectives, because they can't afford his going rates. I am nothing, if not a sentimentalist.

The restaurant was both secluded and exclusive. We sat out on the terrace overlooking the bay. The yachts were out in full force, and the gulls were busy wheeling and dealing in the wide blue yonder. A good day to be alive, and I guessed right now Broderick Rigby would have settled for a rainy day in Manhattan.

"How long were you married?" I asked Melanie.

"Two years," she said, "almost."

"When did it start to go sour?"

"From the beginning, almost," she said. "From the day after the honeymoon, when we moved into the house and I found little sister was already established there."

"And you stuck it how long?"

"Up until four months back," she said, "then I just couldn't take it anymore. So I moved out and filed for divorce on the grounds of mental cruelty. I would have liked to cite little sister as the corespondent, but even my out-of-town lawyer had a small seizure at the thought."

"I know you didn't kill him because I was with you at the time it happened," I said. "So who did?"

"I'd like to think it was Sarah, but if she was going to kill anybody it would have been me." She shrugged. "I honestly don't know who could have wanted to kill Broderick. I mean, he was a useless kind of character. Ineffectual. He never really *did* anything. He went through all the motions, and people were nice to him because of his position and family background. But Sarah was always the brains of the family. She handled the real estate deals and everything."

"You're a big help," I said.

"I know, and I'm sorry," she said coolly. "You know, it's a funny thing, Danny, but from the moment we started talking money, you've become a different person."

"I've become a detective," I said. "That means asking a whole raft of questions, okay?"

She shrugged listlessly. "Okay."

"Was he faithful?"

"As far as I know."

"Were you?"

"Up until the time I moved out," she said. "There were a couple of what you might call minor incidents afterward, but no real relationships."

"Insomnia," I said. "I remember you telling me last night. Sometimes, you said, sex is the only possible answer."

40

"Is my private life going to be a big help to you in finding who killed Broderick?" she asked coldly.

"Who knows?" I said. "There was always a chance some jealous lover just couldn't bear the thought of your husband still being alive."

"Now I'm beginning to worry about you," she said. "I mean, are you a private detective for real? Or just somebody who works out his fantasies by pretending to be a detective?"

"The real estate business," I said. "Anything there?"

"I don't think so," she said. "If there was, it would have been more logical for Sarah to have gotten herself murdered. Like I told you, she was the real brains behind the deals. Broderick was always the figurehead, at best."

"I guess we might as well eat," I said, and picked up the menu.

We left the restaurant around three and drove back to Santo Bahia. Melanie dropped me at my office and went on to her cottage. The atmosphere was still kind of frigid when she left, and she just grunted when I said I would be in touch. I checked out Charles Gray in the phone book and found his office was only a couple of blocks away, so I got reckless and walked. It was a two-story clapboard house, well-weathered, and stuck between a modern boutique on one side, and a quaint ye olde tea shoppe on the other. A kind of reverse status symbol, I guessed—the old-established who not only disdained to move with the times, but had absolutely no need to prove anything. I walked into ye olde office, and a brisk receptionist gave me a professional smile. She was around forty, I figured, neatly dressed, and attractive in an aseptic kind of a way. Maybe she had been bred out of a long line of television moms who coped so gallantly

41

with all those screaming kids, and were so popular a few years back. They always looked like they had given up sex for sewing at the advanced age of thirty, and had never looked back. This one was no exception.

"Good afternoon," she said. "May I help you?"

"I want to see Gray," I said.

Her smile faded. "Mr. Gray is very busy right now," she said. "Do you have an appointment?"

"Just tell him Danny Boyd is here," I said, "and I've brought my mouth with me."

"I'm afraid Mr. Gray never sees anyone without a prior appointment," she said.

"I'll wait," I said.

"It's . . . it's not convenient," she said.

"Maybe there's a back office?" I leered at her. "You know? Someplace where we won't be disturbed, and we can have a little fun while we're waiting?"

Her face was suddenly a deep pink color. "Why, Mr. Boyd," she said in a low voice, "it just so happens we do have a back office, with its very own couch, and everything. If you'll just give me a couple of minutes, I'll slip out of my girdle and—"

"Okay!" I held up my hands in mock surrender. "You win."

She grinned broadly. "I found it very refreshing," she said easily. "You have no idea how many mealy-mouthed old farts I get in here every day."

"Is that a fact, Mrs.—?"

"Eleanor Townsend," she said. "I'm a widow, Mr. Boyd. Not the grieving type any more, because my husband died around six years back. I don't wear a girdle, either. They chafe, especially in Southern California. It's the climate, you know."

"You look so goddamned aseptic," I said, by way of an explanation.

"When you work for a prick like Charles Gray, you don't have much choice," she said, and I wondered if something had happened to my hearing. "But evenings, and weekends, it's different. I let my hair down, throw away the cast-iron bra, and bounce around just like the rest of the girls. I'm an immutable thirty-six, and that makes me a girl, if you see what I mean? You're the first real live man I've seen around here in a coon's age, and I guess that's why I'm talking like this. Bawdy, and all. But it's been so long since I've had a good screw, I can hardly remember. I hope you don't think I'm being forward, or anything, Mr. Boyd?"

"Uh!" I said.

"He's not doing anything right now," she said, and her voice was suddenly professional again, and maybe tinged with disappointment. "So why don't you just walk right in on him? I can always say you brushed me aside like some old flame."

"A thirty-six-year-old flame should burn real bright," I said.

"Catch me after dark on a couch and you'll be dazzled," she said. "The second door to your right, Mr. Boyd."

Charles Gray was sitting at his desk doing exactly nothing when I walked in on him. He looked up at me and his expression didn't change at all.

"You're supposed to make an appointment," he said. "Or have my secretary announce you. You could have at least knocked before walking in here."

"Your secretary tried real hard to stop me from coming in here," I lied.

"All right," he said. "What do you want, Boyd?"

"Melanie Rigby's hired me to find out who killed her husband," I said. "I figured you could help."

"You lied to us last night," he said. "Captain Schell told us about it this morning when Sarah identified the body for him. You were both there, up at the cabin last night."

"But we didn't kill him," I said.

"I don't think I should talk with you, Boyd," he said. "Sarah Rigby is an old and valued client of mine, and she is convinced you and Melanie killed her brother."

"And what do you think?"

"I'm a lawyer," he said. "I never jump to conclusions."

"Who gets the money?" I asked him.

"A most improper question, Mr. Boyd."

"Who wanted him dead?"

"You know, I really think you should talk with Sarah," he said. "I'm always inhibited in my professional capacity. Sarah is never inhibited."

"Bully for Sarah," I said.

"You exude a certain crude vitality she might find quite interesting," he said. "It was certainly lacking last night, Mr. Boyd. But then you had other things on your mind, of course, like trying to sustain the lie, and already knowing Broderick Rigby had been brutally done to death. I'll call her now and make an appointment for you if you like?"

"Why not?" I said.

He dialed the number and I tried not to fidget while I listened to the one-sided conversation. It's moments like these, since I quit smoking, that I just don't know what the hell to do. Finally he hung up, and looked at me again.

"Nine tonight," he said. "After dinner, of course."

"Where do I find her?"

"The house is on Sublime Point," he said. "My secretary can give you the details."

"Fine," I said.

"Does Captain Schell know Melanie has hired you to find out who murdered Broderick?"

"I don't think so," I said carefully.

"Perhaps somebody should tell him." He smiled at me. "Good day, Mr. Boyd."

"Bobo Shanks," I said. "What does he do?"

"I don't think I understand the question?"

"I'm a private detective," I said. "You're a lawyer. What is Bobo Shanks?"

"I think you'd better ask him that question," he said. "Good day, Mr. Boyd."

Eleanor Townsend was sitting at her desk looking thoughtful when I got back to the outer office.

"He says you can tell me where to find the Rigby house up on Sublime Point," I said.

"I'll even draw you a dinky little diagram," she said, and did.

"Thanks," I told her, and put the diagram into my wallet. "He doesn't look like he's real busy."

"He very rarely is," she said, "busy. When you work with the top families of Santo Bahia—and with whom you share a common background—you don't work too hard. It's more like you collect the retainers, you know. And when somebody starts throwing stinking fish, you come right out of left field and throw them back."

"The Rigby family?" I said.

"Mr. Boyd," she said briskly, "I simply wouldn't know. It's like I told you, I don't wear a girdle because they chafe in a hot climate."

"Huh?" I said blankly.

"That Sarah Rigby," she said. "I bet she never wore a girdle in her whole life."

"But she wears Charles Gray just in case somebody starts throwing stinking fish?"

"There's a man called Hy Adams lives in this town," she said. "You're new here so you never heard of him, right?"

"Right," I said.

"Maybe you should go talk with him sometime," she said. "But don't forget to wear your cast-iron girdle when you do, because the heat can get to be something awful around him."

"I wish I knew what the hell you're talking about," I said truthfully.

"Mr. Gray left the intercom open in his office just now," she said. "Whenever he does it, it's deliberate so he's got me as a witness if anything should come of it. The widow-lady's hired you to find out who killed her husband, so I heard. Hy Adams did a lot of business with her late husband and I think you should go talk with him. But watch your back while you're doing it."

"Thanks," I said.

"Us aseptic girls have to find our fun someplace," she said easily. "I mean, we can always go ride a horse bareback but what kind of fun is that for the horse?"

"You have a lot of class, Eleanor," I said. "The way you casually threw in that 'whom' back there. It isn't easy. How about we have dinner tomorrow night?"

"You're just saying that because you figure you can pry some more information out of me," she said.

"Pry!" I said, admiringly. "You're absolutely right. I sure hope I can pry some more information out of you, Eleanor. Like I already know you don't wear a girdle because they chafe in the Southern California climate, but now I'm getting this irresistible urge to find out if you're wearing anything at all underneath that real plain cotton dress."

"Oh, my!" she said in a fluttering voice. "You're so romantic, Mr. Boyd, I could swoon at your feet just listening to your voice. The Luau Bar in the Starlight Hotel tomorrow night around seven. And I warn you, I don't sell myself cheaply. I'll insist on eating from the à la carte menu!"

Chapter Five

There was this dump that specialized in pancakes and I made the big mistake of eating there. So by the time I arrived at the Rigby residence up on Sublime Point, I had indigestion to add to my other troubles. The house was grandiose, perched close to the cliff edge, and designed by some crazy Spaniard with delusions of architecture, I suspected. I parked the car on the gravel drive and walked up onto the front porch. Muted chimes played someplace inside the house and I waited around twenty seconds before the door opened. Then Sarah Rigby was standing there looking at me down the length of her nose. She was wearing a floor-length dress made out of clinging white jersey which emphasized her trim athletic figure and the fact that she wasn't wearing a bra.

"Good evening, Mr. Boyd," she said. "You won't forget to wipe your feet, will you?"

I walked into the front hall and she closed the door in back of me.

"We'll go into the living room and have a drink," she said. "Liquor and fornication are the two prime movers in a private detective's life, I believe."

"You're absolutely right, Miss Rigby," I told her,

"and I would prefer a bourbon on the rocks before we start fornicating, if that's okay with you?"

She made an outraged snorting sound, then led the way into the living room. The material of her dress stretched tightly over her undulating bottom as she sashayed into the room, which was furnished in a kind of early hacienda style, with everything looking real uncomfortable. In the daytime, the view through the French doors would have been fantastic, I guessed, but on a moonless night there was nothing but blackness out there. Bobo Shanks was sitting comfortably in an armchair with a drink in his right hand, and he gave me an affable wave with his free hand.

"Hi!" he said, like we were old buddies already.

Sarah Rigby went over to the bar and made my drink, then gave it to me.

"Do sit down, Mr. Boyd," she said.

So I sat down on the couch while she sat down in another armchair, and then the three of us just looked at each other.

"Charles said on the phone that Melanie has hired you to find my brother's murderer," she said for openers. "Is that correct, Mr. Boyd?"

"That's right," I agreed.

"And why did you wish to see me?"

"Somebody had a motive for killing your brother," I said. "You were real close to him, Melanie says, so maybe you'd know that somebody."

"The obvious choice is Melanie herself," she said.

"Sure," I said. "But I was with her last night from around seven-thirty on, and I know she didn't kill him."

"So you say, Mr. Boyd!"

"You ran the business," I said. "Your brother was only the figurehead, right?"

"More gems of wisdom from dear Melanie?"

"Okay," I said. "You were very close to your brother, then Melanie married him, and, from that moment on, the both of you hated each other. Melanie would like to believe you killed him, but she has enough logic left to admit that if you were about to kill anybody it would have been her."

Shanks chuckled, then stopped suddenly as the brunette froze him with one look.

"Melanie's right about that, anyway," she said. "She came very close to destroying my brother, flaunting her wanton affairs with other men right under his nose. But I guess she hasn't told you about them."

"She hasn't told me much about anything," I said. "Why don't we start with a basic premise that neither you nor Melanie killed your brother, and that both of you want to find out who did kill him?"

"I'm afraid your word that Melanie didn't kill him isn't enough for me, Mr. Boyd," she said icily.

"Sarah," Shanks said softly. "Why don't you hear the man out?"

"Who the hell asked you?" she snapped.

"You did, as I remember."

"All right," she said. "So come to the point, Mr. Boyd."

"Whoever killed him must have had good reason from their own viewpoint," I said.

"I don't have any idea who could have wanted to kill my brother," she said wearily. "If I had, I would have most certainly told Captain Schell."

"When he asked Melanie to meet him at the cabin, he said it was a secret between the both of them," I said, "but he obviously told you about it."

"He was hoping to make Melanie see reason about the size of the divorce settlement," she said. "He thought if they met where they had spent their honeymoon, perhaps it would help."

"Who else did he tell?"

"I don't know," she said flatly. "I told him he was being stupid and sentimental. But I couldn't dissuade him from going. After he left I called Charles and Bobo, and asked them over here. When Broderick didn't return, I thought he must have still been with Melanie, and that's why the three of us visited the cottage. We didn't expect to find Melanie there, to be truthful. I thought the both of them were still probably up at the log cabin, and Broderick might have been stupid enough to try and effect a reconciliation."

"You can't think of any reason why anybody would have wanted your brother dead?" I said.

"None," she said, "as I've already told you, Mr. Boyd."

"Well," I got up onto my feet, "thanks for the drink, anyway."

"You're leaving already, Mr. Boyd?" she said.

"Melanie's no help," I said, "and neither are you. So I guess I'll have to go look someplace else."

"I'm glad you reminded me, Mr. Boyd," she said. "It is my considered opinion that the police are perfectly capable of finding my brother's murderer. The name Rigby is a well-respected one in Santo Bahia, and I have no intention of allowing it to be cheapened by some dirty little peephole artist like yourself bandying it about. You'll drop the whole thing as of now, Mr. Boyd. If you wish to continue living here, that is."

"Are you threatening me, Miss Rigby?" I asked politely.

"I most certainly am," she said. "The investigation can be safely left to Captain Schell and his men. I have every faith in them. I suggest that from now on you concentrate on divorce, or whatever charming specialty you have, Mr. Boyd."

"And if I don't?"

"A whole series of nasty accidents, old buddy," Shanks said casually. "And nobody in Santo Bahia—and I do include Schell in this—will believe they are anything else."

"I'm flattered," I said. "I worry you this much already?"

"I'm only worried about the family name and reputation," the brunette said. "Just drop it, Mr. Boyd, and who knows—you may live to enjoy a long and happy life in Santo Bahia."

"You've both got to be very sure of yourselves," I said. "I mean, like no sweetener?"

"Sweetener?" she said.

"I guess he's operating by his usual standards," Shanks said. "He's talking about a bribe."

"There's no need for a bribe, I can assure you, Mr. Boyd." Sarah Rigby smiled thinly at me. "There are a hundred different ways in which we can make your life unbearable here, if you insist."

"There is one thing before I go," I said pleasantly. "The way I hear it, you and your brother had a real close relationship. So close, it was almost like a marriage of its own. Is that right, Miss Rigby?"

"Get out!" Her face was a chalky-white color. "Get out, you hear?" Her eyes were taking on a glazed look as she stared at me. "You filthy-minded little bastard! I'll—I'll—get *out!*"

"I'll make damned sure he goes, and right now," Shanks said determinedly.

The old adage is often the best adage—like, never give a sucker an even break. So I moved real fast and clobbered him while he was still only halfway out of his chair, and completely defenseless. I sank my right fist deep into his solar plexus, then, as he bent forward, brought my knee sharply up into his face. He was flung back into the chair, the blood spurting from his mashed nose, and I took the opportunity to hit him straight between the eyes. From then on, he just wasn't interested.

I turned around in time to see Sarah Rigby coming straight at me, her eyes spitting fury, and her fingers hooked into talons ready to rip into my face. I was in no mood to reason with her right then, and judging from the way she looked, with her eyeballs still glazed, she was in no mood to listen to reason, either. So I let her get close, then booted her right shinbone real hard. She let out a frantic scream, then went hopping around the room in a wide circle, like a winged duck that can't make up its mind if it should risk a forced landing.

"And that," I said as I started toward the door, "is only the first in a whole series of nasty accidents to come!"

I went back to the car and started the drive home. About halfway I decided that maybe I had been just a little bit of a bastard to Melanie at the restaurant, so I turned the car around and headed toward Paradise Beach. The lights were on inside the cottage and I rang the doorbell confidently. She took a hell of a long time to answer and I was starting to grow old by the time she finally opened the front door. She was wearing an itty-bitty black silk robe, with a hem that barely reached the top of her firm thighs. If she could only stretch herself the tiniest fraction, I would be able to see if she was wearing panties beneath it. Her loose breasts were heavy beneath the black silk. She looked like it was taking a big effort to keep her eyes open, and her face had a puffiness that went with her swollen lips.

"Oh," she said, with no enthusiasm at all. "It's you. You woke me up."

"You went to sleep with all the lights on?"

"I was tired," she said, and yawned loudly. The robe lifted a fraction, but not quite enough to answer the burning question of the moment. "What do you want, Danny?"

"I figured I should apologize," I said. "I guess I wasn't exactly a lot of laughs at lunchtime."

"Okay," she said. "You apologized. Thanks." Then she started to close the door.

"Hey," I said. "Not even a drink?"

"I'm sorry, Danny." She yawned again, even louder. "I'm just so goddamned tired, I can hardly keep my eyes open."

"Melanie!" a deep bass voice bellowed from the bedroom. "Are you going to stand there yakking all night, or are you coming back to bed?"

"You never told me your sister was visiting," I said coldly.

"Oh, shit!" she said, then blinked at me doubtfully. "He's an old friend."

"Last night I was a new friend in your bed," I said. "How long have you known him? Since the night before last?"

"Oh, shit!" she said again.

"Melanie!" the deep bass voice bellowed again.

"Ah, shut up!" I bellowed right back.

"I wish I were dead," Melanie said, and closed her eyes tight shut.

I saw him coming over her shoulder, with a towel knotted around his waist. A big bull of a guy, bald on

54

top, with bright red hair around the edges. His face and neck sported a deep tan, a sharp contrast to the whiteness of his torso. The mustache was thick and red, and the eyes were a light blue and set close together.

"This is Hy Adams," Melanie said, "and I wish I was dead."

"Hi, Adams," I said.

"Who the fuck are you?" he bellowed.

"Danny Boyd," I said. "Didn't anybody ever tell you to take off your shirt when you get into the sun?"

He put his hands around Melanie's waist, lifted her a couple of feet up into the air, and now the black silk robe rode right up over her stomach, confirming my guess that she was wearing nothing beneath it. There was a brief glimpse of yellow hair and meshing pink as she kicked her legs, and then he put her down again in back of him. She opened her mouth to say something, then changed her mind.

"You wish you were dead?" I said helpfully.

"I'm a reasonable man, Boyd," Adams thundered. "You came visiting at the wrong moment, okay? So get lost."

It sounded reasonable, and I was a resonable man, I told myself. So I had gotten into bed with Melanie the previous night, but the circumstances were exceptional, to say the least. A momentary desperation on her part, born out of seeing her husband's body swinging on a chandelier with his throat hacked out. Then the added stresses of Sarah Rigby and friends, not to mention Captain Schell. So I was about to say a courteous good night, but then Adams had to go and spoil the whole thing.

"Get the hell out of here, Boyd," he said, "before I take you apart, itty-bitty muscle by itty-bitty muscle!"

If Santo Bahia was ever going to be my town, I figured I just couldn't walk away from that kind of statement.

"Melanie," I said in an urgent voice. "Don't use that knife on him. He isn't worth it."

I figured Adams had to be the kind of a guy who never trusted anybody, and I was proved right. He spun around real fast, presenting his back to me. A hop, a skip, and then I booted him in the tail with all the force I could find. It was like he was suddenly jet-propelled. He shot forward, cannoned into Melanie, and knocked her flat. Her legs shot up in the air as he fell forward on top of her, and there was another flash of the pink meshing flash between her curved thighs. She was wide awake, I could see that clearly. Dying, by the desperate look in her eyes, but wide awake.

"Sixty bucks for the lunch and drinks," I said, "plus the original two hundred you owe me for last night. Just put a check in the mail, huh? I wouldn't want to be seen dead with a client like you."

She opened her mouth and, for a moment there, I figured she was about to say something. Then I realized she was just trying to get some air back into her lungs. With Adams' whole weight lying on top of her, I guessed it wasn't easy. Adams made a big decision, to get up off Melanie. So he raised himself up on his hands and knees for a start. There was a deep whooping noise as Melanie finally got some air back into her lungs. The knotted towel had slipped sideways, and the bare butt was too much of a temptation. So I booted it again, knocking Adams flat. There was another deep whooping sound as the air was rapidly expelled out of Melanie's lungs. What the hell? I thought. We could go on like this for the rest of the night. So I stepped back onto the front porch and slammed the door shut in back of me. Then I stood to one side and waited. It took around fifteen seconds before the door opened again and a naked Adams came charging out into the night. I lifted a stiffened right leg. His knees hit it, then he looped off the front tucking my legs up underneath me, and my knees hit his kidneys as I landed on his back. The air came whistling out of his lungs, and then he just lay there. I put one hand under his chin, gripped the back of his neck with the other, then twisted his head around painfully.

"The name is Boyd," I said evenly. "The next time we tangle I'll twist your itty-bitty head clean off your itty-bitty shoulders."

I got back up onto my feet and started walking toward the car. What the hell I had proved I didn't know, exactly, but I certainly felt a hell of a lot better. I was about to open the car door when a voice croaked, "Danny!" When I looked around, I saw Melanie standing on the front porch. She had lost her black silk robe someplace in the struggle, but it didn't seem to matter, somehow. That classical female form, shimmering palely in the light, I could take or leave right now.

"He'll kill you after this," she said. "You don't know him the way I do!"

"What do you care?" I said.

"Danny! I need you!" she wailed. "I'll mail that check in the morning, plus the thousand for your expenses. We still have a deal. Just so you don't let Hy kill you before you've found out who killed Broderick."

"Okay," I said, "but add an extra five hundred to the check."

"For what?"

"Above and beyond the call of duty," I said. "Sleeping with you, you bitch, last night."

"You can go screw yourself!" she yelled.

"Good-bye, Melanie," I told her, and started to get into the car.

"Danny!" she wailed, in a high tremolo. "How much is that altogether?"

"Seventeen hundred and sixty dollars," I said.

"You're a miserable bastard!"

"Next time you have a problem, just don't call me," I said.

"I'll put a check in the mail first thing in the morning," she said frantically.

"There's one other thing," I said. "If it's proved he was a suicide, you don't get your money back. Not a nickel!"

She was just starting to scream when I got into the car and drove away.

Chapter Six

I got there early the next morning, around a quarter of nine, because I figured she would never be late. A long five minutes went by and then I saw her coming down the street. She was wearing a real neat blouse with a high collar buttoned right up to the neck, and a severe skirt that reached her knees, with each pleat precisely in place. Her dark brown hair was severely brushed, with not one hair out of place. She looked attractive, wholesome, and completely sexless. But I knew better, I hoped, as I walked across the street to intercept her.

"Good day, Mrs. Townsend," I said. "A beautiful day, is it not?"

"Just a typical Santo Bahia day, Mr. Boyd," she said. "For the first couple of months here you'll be ecstatic over each successive beautiful morning, then you'll get used to them, and then you'll start praying for a hurricane or anything to break the goddamned monotony of it all."

"It's too good a day to waste in an office," I said. "Too bad you've suddenly developed this migraine."

"The Luau Bar tonight," she said. "Isn't that the time for our date?"

"It was," I said, "but I need you right now, Eleanor."

"Not right here on the sidewalk, Danny," she said demurely. "I don't want to wind up with a fried fanny."

"I need your help," I said. "I need to get out of town for the day, and I need information. Three people are going to start looking for me anytime now, with nothing but mayhem and probably murder on their minds."

"Would I know them?"

"Sarah Rigby, Bobo Shanks, and Hy Adams," I said.

"You've met Adams?"

"I kicked him in the butt last night," I said.

"Oh, my!" She shook her head slowly. "The only advice I can give you is run for your life and don't stop until you hit the East Coast."

"How about that migraine?" I said.

"Okay," she said. "What have I got to lose except my job, and my sanity."

"My car's parked a block down the street," I said as I started walking beside her.

"We should go back to my place first," she said. "So I can call Mr. Gray, and then change. What kind of a day did you have in mind, Danny?"

"A real lazy day," I said. "A drive out to someplace with a beach and a good restaurant."

"It sounds nice," she said. "I feel like telling Mr. Gray what he can do with his torts and estoppels, but I guess a migraine is safer."

Her place was a small house on a street of small houses on the unfashionable side of Santo Bahia, away from the ocean, and, I guessed, the kind of place where most of the workers in Santo Bahia lived. She left me in the living room while she made her call, and I looked out the window at the trim lawn, the shrubs, and the riot of flowers. Her head reappeared around the door for a moment.

"I'll get changed, then I'll make some coffee, okay?" she said.

"Fine," I told her. "How was Mr. Gray?"

"Solicitous," she said, then chuckled gleefully before her head vanished again.

So I went back to the window again. After what seemed a long time I heard her voice in back of me.

"Danny?" she said hesitantly.

I turned around and found she was only a few feet away from me. She was barefoot, and that was why I hadn't heard her come into the room. She was not only barefoot, she was mostly bare, wearing only an itty-bitty black bikini. Her figure was superb. The full, deep breasts swept boldly down into the small cups of the bikini top, and there was only the gentlest curve to her belly. Her legs were firm and rounded. She had brushed out her hair, wiped off the obligatory makeup, and looked at least ten years younger.

"Wow!" I said respectfully.

"Wow?" Her dark brown eyes looked at me carefully. "Is that your considered opinion?"

"Wow!" I nodded vigorously.

"I'm glad," she said. "I figured it was only fair you should see me first. So you didn't have to be saddled with a sex-hungry old hag for the rest of the day, just so you could get what you wanted."

"I'm not sure I can wait all day to get what I want," I said truthfully.

She grinned widely. "I was talking about information," she said. "You want some coffee?"

"If we stop for coffee it will mean rape," I said. "The choice is yours."

"I don't think we'll stop for coffee," she said. "It's not the rape I'm objecting to, but I want the day you've promised me first."

Then she got dressed to go out. A denim skirt that just reached the middle of her thighs, and a thin cotton top. Somehow, after she had put them on, she looked even more undressed. We went out to the car and I asked her where we were going.

"South," she said. "There's one beach I know that doesn't get too crowded, even in mid-season."

It was a great beach. We swam, lazed in the sun, then swam some more. We had a fantastic lunch at the clifftop restaurant, went back to the beach and slept it off, then swam some more. Around six in the evening, Eleanor said it was time we were going.

"I need a shower, Danny," she said, "and I know just the place for dinner and, by some strange coincidence, there's a good motel just a half mile back from the restaurant."

"Why don't we check into the motel first, then you can have your shower," I said.

"We can talk over dinner," she said. "I'm not sure I can help you too much, but I'll certainly try."

"At this stage I don't care," I said. "I'm too busy lusting after your beautiful body."

We checked into the motel, had our showers, then went to the restaurant. The owner had gotten smart. If he couldn't have a seascape, he had obviously figured the hell with it, who needed one, anyway? So he had cunningly landscaped his trees and lawns and shrubs, had backlit them for the nights when the moon wouldn't cooperate, and had placed his tables with great care. Someplace in the middle of the shrubbery a trio of musicians played slow tempo schmaltzy music. It was a great place to linger, especially if you had an attractive woman like Eleanor along with you. When we got to the coffee and cordial stage, Eleanor leaned back in her chair and sighed gently.

"It's been a great day, Danny," she said. "I don't know how to thank you."

"The best is yet to come," I said.

"I hope so." She waved one hand in the air desperately. "What I mean is, I hope I'm right for you, good enough for you."

"What kind of a place is this that plants a sudden inferiority complex in you?" I said.

"Everything's been so perfect, I just don't want to spoil it," she said, "and now is a good time for you to ask for your information, I think!"

So I told her what had happened from the moment Melanie Rigby walked into my office up until the moment I had left her screaming her head off outside the Paradise Beach cottage the previous night. She was a good listener, and she sat in silence after I had finished.

"Maybe Melanie had a motive for killing him," I said, "but I know she didn't kill him, because I was with her the whole evening. So somebody else must have killed him. Who, and why? I figured you could give me some background maybe."

"I'll try," she said. "How well do you know Santo Bahia, Danny?"

"I've been here a few times before," I said. "Working visits. I never stayed that long at any time."

"You know it's a resort town," she said. "The local population makes its living from the tourists. These days, the residents with money make more money out of real estate development. But there's only so much land, and only so much development is possible. So

63

the competition gets real intense. A few of the old wealthy families—like the Rigbys, for example—remained aloof when the boom started. But they soon changed their minds when they saw the kind of money that was being made. And they have a lot going for them. It's a real exclusive league, Danny, where when you want something done, or not done, you just pick up the phone and speak to your old family buddy who happens to be the mayor, or whatever."

"I get the picture," I said.

"Everybody figured Hy Adams was a roughneck who wouldn't last five minutes when he first moved here," she said. "But then they saw how he could move on a development and they changed their minds. They figured on tossing him out, but they'd picked the wrong man. So then they decided if they couldn't beat him, they'd join him."

"The Rigbys?"

"Especially the Rigbys," she said. "Charles Gray is their attorney, and I'm his personal secretary. I don't know too much about their specific dealings with Hy Adams, but I do know they're heavily involved."

"According to Melanie, her husband was only a figurehead," I said, "and Sarah is the business brains of the family."

"I'm sure she's right," Eleanor said. "Whenever they had a meeting with Charles Gray, Sarah was always there. I don't think I ever saw Broderick at more than a couple of the meetings, at most."

"I'd like to see his will," I said.

"Gray keeps it in his safe, and he's the only one who has the combination," she said. "Sorry."

"How about Bobo Shanks?" I said. "What the hell does he do?"

"He comes from one of the old families, too," she said. "He's the mystery man around here. Nobody knows what he does, exactly. For sure, he's loaded with money." She frowned for a moment. "There have been some nasty rumors about him, but nothing you can pin down."

"Like what?"

"A maid at his house who was so badly beaten up she had to have emergency surgery in the middle of the night," she said. "The official story was she'd had an accident—had fallen down the stairs or something. But as soon as she reached the convalescent stage, she left town. The same rumor said Shanks paid her off to keep her mouth shut. There have been others. He got involved in a bar fight one night and nearly killed a man, but he was only a no-account tourist and everybody who saw the fight swore he was drunk and had started it."

She smiled at me. "I'm really scraping the bottom of the barrel, Danny."

"Keep going," I told her.

"Talk of goings-on up at his house, sex orgies, and the like. The women brought in from out of town, and sent back again the next morning."

"Does he invite his friends to the orgies, or are they staged just for his own enjoyment?" I asked her.

"He supposedly invites his friends," she said lightly. "All his rich upper-crust friends, who else?"

"Including the Rigbys?"

"I guess so," she said. "I've never heard their names actually mentioned. In fact, come to think of it, I've only ever heard one name mentioned, Hy Adams. Some of the nastier gossip says that's how they got to make a deal with him, by providing him with some very specialized entertainment."

"Where is his house?"

"Real close to the Rigby house, where you were last night," she said. "A quarter mile away, at most."

"And he was with Melanie last night," I said. "Maybe I should ask her if she's been to any good orgies lately?"

"Talking of orgies," she said softly, "isn't it about time we went back to the motel?"

It was a nice motel suite, as motel suites go, but I never did get to see that much of it. As soon as we got back there, Eleanor went straight into the bedroom, and closed the door in back of her. I settled down for a long wait and it lasted less than a minute. The door opened again and Eleanor's head peeked around it.

"You mean, you've still got your clothes on?" She sniffed disdainfully. "What are you, the shy kind of a rapist?"

I got out of my clothes real fast, then walked quickly into the bedroom. Eleanor was lying on the bed, her naked body waiting to welcome me. Now that I could see it for what it was, I must say her body exceeded all my expectations. It was firm and ripe, her breasts rising and falling in gentle expectation. Her lips were parted and there was a hungry look in her eyes. One leg was straight, the other was raised. Her hands were clasped behind her head.

"Hi there," I said, and my prick gave a little wave of greeting as well.

"Hi, yourself." She lowered her leg, and raised the other one, then unclasping her hands from behind her head, held them up to me.

Responding, I moved across to her. By now, my yard was fully erect. I sat down on the bed beside her. She sat up, and placing her hands on my shoulders, eased me down onto my back. Then, before I could do anything about it, she was lying on top of me, kissing me, nuzzling me, working her way down my body. I lay there, and let her take the initiative. The tips of her teeth worried my nipples a little, and her tongue darted into my navel. She raised her head and smiled at me. I winked back at her. Her hand closed around my rearing, twitching staff, and then as her head lowered to it, I could feel the cool caress of her lips deftly bringing it to a state of even greater awareness. While she was doing this, her fingers lightly massaged my testicles.

I took about as much of this as I could stand, then sitting up, I eased her head away from my prick, and hauled her back up onto the bed beside me. Now, I thought, it was my turn, so I went through the same ritual with her, feeling the rubberiness of her breasts in my mouth as my teeth bit gently into her nipples, and her body began to rock and heave beneath me; and the faint saltiness as my lips brushed against her hair-covered mound. With my hands holding her legs apart, I dived in between them, all caution gone to the winds, my tongue prising the lips of her vagina apart, laving the smooth, sensitive flesh, prodding her clitoris, and I heard her moans as if from a great cavernous distance. Her body was rocking more violently, her fingers clutched my hair, and she kept repeating my name over and over again. Then I looked at her. Her stomach rose and fell with her heavy breathing. She held up her hands.

"Come on, Danny Boyd," she breathed. "What are you waiting for?"

I brought myself up on top of her, sliding my body in between her drawn-up legs, my rod slipping easily into her warm, moist, snugly enclosing sheath.

We pumped each other dry. Our bodies hammered against each other, and there was the sound of wetly slapping flesh as we drove each other to the limits of endurance. Eleanor's legs were clamped tightly around my body, and she shouted crude obscenities in my ears. We reached a simultaneous climax that knocked all the breath from my body, and which made Eleanor cry out in sheer ecstasy. Even so, as her body shuddered with each successive wave of sensation, her contracted vaginal muscles held me in a tight, viselike grip.

"Danny," she whispered. "I could die content right now. I've never been so happy in my whole life before."

Then the delicious post-coital drowsiness crept up on us and we went to sleep.

I woke up suddenly in the early hours of the morning because I figured I had heard a noise, then was about to go back to sleep when I heard it again. A soft sound, like the scraping of a shoe on the floor. Eleanor was still sleeping deeply beside me when I sat up in the bed. Then a flashlight beam hit me straight in the eyes and momentarily blinded me. I got one foot onto the floor before something hit me across the back of the head with savage force, and the whole world exploded into darkness.

When I woke up again, daylight was beginning to filter in through the windows. My head felt like it had been split in two, and it took one hell of an effort to lift it. I sat up slowly, and tenderly probed the back of my head with my fingers. There was a small area that felt a little mushy and hurt like hell to the touch. A blow from a gun butt? I wondered. Then I realized the rest of the bed was empty. I checked the bathroom and the living room. Eleanor had gone, and her clothes had gone with her. It was like she had never been there. I could have gotten dressed and rushed off in all directions to look for her, but the chances of finding her that way were remote, I figured. And my head was still pounding, so I figured the hell with it and went back to bed.

Chapter Seven

I got back to my office around eleven the same morning. On the way there I had stopped at Eleanor's house and had rung the doorbell a half dozen times. Nobody had answered. Five minutes after I had gotten back into the office the phone rang.

"Danny!" Melanie's voice wailed. "Where the hell have you been?"

"Working," I lied.

"I've called you a million times," she said. "Did you get my check?"

I looked at the small pile of unopened mail I'd brought in with me. "I guess so," I said.

"When Hy Adams catches up with you, he's going to kill you," she said. "I thought you should know."

"Thanks for telling me."

"Captain Schell came around yesterday afternoon and asked me a million questions. I'm not sure he really believes us about what happened up at the cabin, Danny."

"Schell usually doesn't believe anything anybody tells him," I said. "He figures everybody lies to a cop because they figure he wouldn't believe them if they told him the truth, anyway."

"What?" she said doubtfully.

"I'm writing a book about it," I said. "Psychosomatics says you are what you think you are. My book's about coposomatics, and it says you are what a cop thinks you are. My guess is it should sell five copies, maybe six, even."

"I wish you'd stop it," she said plaintively. "My brain's beginning to hurt. When am I going to see you?"

"When I've got something to report," I said. "I don't have anything right now."

"I'm lonely," she said. "Why don't you come out here and have lunch with me?"

"Why don't you ask Hy Adams?"

"I can explain about him," she said quickly, "but not over the phone. Do you like lobster, Danny? I'll fix some lobster and a green salad, and I'll made my special dessert for you, and I'll get some wine, too. You do like wine, Danny?"

"What time?"

"About one," she said. "I'll whip up a bunch of martinis, too."

"Great," I said, and my head throbbed as I put down the phone.

I dialed the number of Gray's office and a female voice answered. When I asked to talk with Mrs. Townsend, the voice said she was out sick. So I hung up again. If they had kidnapped Eleanor from the motel, they obviously had a reason. And if the reason was me, I would hear from them. It was a barren kind of logic but I couldn't do any better right then.

When I parked the car out front of the cottage at Paradise Beach, the front door opened almost before I had time to cut the motor, and Melanie came running joyfully toward me. She was wearing a black cotton

71

top and white shorts that were caught up tightly around her crotch, and everything was bouncing every which way as she ran. I got out of the car and she charged straight into me, flinging her arms around my neck. Her boobs were soft and yielding against my manly chest.

"Danny!" she said. "It's so good to see you again!"

"Six months in a frozen white hell," I said, "but the North Pole is like that."

"What?"

"It's only been around thirty-six hours," I said. "You can't have missed me that much."

"I've missed you," she said. "I cried myself to sleep last night, I was so lonely without you." She pulled away from me. "It's another woman, isn't it?"

"What the hell are you talking about?"

"It's obvious," she said. "You're just not interested in me anymore."

My head was starting to throb again, so I walked past her into the living room of the cottage. The shaker was standing on the bar, so I made myself a generous martini, then took an appreciative sip. Melanie slammed the front door shut in back of her, then stood glaring at me with her hands on her hips.

"Who is she?" she demanded.

"An Italian countess," I said. "We spent the night together at her villa on Capri. It was a fantastic experience, but when you're tied to scheduled flights, it doesn't leave you much time to relax."

"All right, Danny." She smiled thinly. "So maybe there isn't any other woman and I was just being stupid. I hate sex first thing in the morning, and maybe sex at lunchtime doesn't interest you, either. Right?"

"Right," I said.

"So where were you all day yesterday, and last night?"

"Out of Santo Bahia," I said. "I tangled with Sarah Rigby and Bobo Shanks before I tangled with Hy Adams the night before last. So it seemed like a good idea to get out of town for a while and let everybody cool off a little."

"You tangled with Sarah and Bobo!" Her eyes brightened with curiosity. "What happened?"

I told her what had happened. She liked the bit about me beating up Shanks, but she liked the bit about me clobbering Sarah on the shin a hell of a lot more.

"Oh, Danny!" Her violet eyes were shining. "I wish I'd been there to see it."

"So, there I was," I said. "Busy clobbering the both of them, and meanwhile, back at the cottage, you were in bed with Hy Adams."

"It's hard to explain." She walked across to the bar and helped herself to a drink. "He's a hard man to refuse."

"You mean he raped you?" I said derisively, looking her six feet of well-proportioned body up and down. "Little you?"

"No!" She flushed angrily. "I didn't mean that. But I was in a low mood and still kind of unstrung after what happened the previous night. It just didn't seem worth arguing about, is all. And who the hell are you to criticize, anyway?"

"It wasn't the first time?"

"No, not that it's any of your goddamned business."

"Adams was your lover?"

She shook her head quickly. "It just happened a couple of times while I was married, is all. Nothing significant. Hy Adams has had just about every woman in town. The ones he wanted, I mean. And if their husbands find out, they ignore it because they're either afraid of him physically, or afraid of not doing business with him any more."

"Which category did Broderick fall into?"

"Broderick never knew," she said. "Anyway, let's change the subject, Danny. I'm getting goddamned bored with this crap!"

"Where would I find Adams?"

"You want to be careful he doesn't find you!"

"Where would I find him?"

"He has an office in town," she said. "Adams Constructions, Inc., and it's in the phone book. You can always find him there."

"What does Bobo Shanks do?" I asked her.

"I don't think he does anything much," she said. "He's rich. I guess he lives off his investments."

"What does he do for fun?"

"Fun?" She shrugged. "I wouldn't know. Sarah, maybe, but I doubt it. She never had time for another man, not while Broderick was still alive, anyway."

"I picked up a rumor about Shanks," I said carefully. "He's an orgy man."

"You're kidding!"

"A maid at his house who was so badly beaten up she had to have emergency surgery in the middle of the night," I said. "He nearly killed a guy in a bar fight, but the guy was only a no-account tourist. Then there are the women brought in from out of town specially for the orgies, and sent back again in the morning."

"I've heard some crazy rumors in my time," Melanie said, "but that's the wildest one yet!"

"The same rumor says the orgies are staged for his friends," I said. "Members of the upper-crust families.

It was how they got into partnership with Hy Adams, by inviting him along to the orgies and giving him some real unique entertainment."

"Whoever started that rumor has one hell of an imagination," she said tightly. "One hell of a real dirty imagination!"

"If it was true, you'd know about it, right?"

"I'm not sure I would," she said, "but I'm sure it isn't true. Just what is it you're implying, Danny?"

"I'm implying I'd like to believe you," I said, "and maybe I would if I hadn't walked in on you and Hy Adams. You were enjoying it, baby!"

"Is there some kind of law against enjoying it?"

"I guess not," I said. "You want to know something, Melanie? For a client who hired me to find out who murdered her husband, you're about as much help as a prime suspect."

"So maybe we should forget the whole thing," she said in a brittle voice. "Okay?"

"We still have a deal," I said. "I haven't spent all that expense money yet."

"Suddenly, I'm not hungry," she said. "So I guess we can forget lunch. Will you just get the hell out of here and leave me alone!"

"Sure," I said. "Thanks for the drink."

The moment after I reached the front porch, the door slammed shut in back of me. I had a quick lunch at a fast-food chicken place and was real glad they didn't serve pancakes, right up until I tasted the first mouthful of their chicken. It was around two-thirty in the afternoon when I got back to my office. Her check was there in the unopened mail I had left behind me. I walked it across the street to the bank and asked them to make a special clearance on it. Then, with all my fingers crossed that Melanie didn't stop payment before the check had been cleared, I went back to my office. The phone book said Adams Constructions, Inc., had an office on Vista Street, which was about four blocks away. I dialed the number and asked to speak with Adams. Mr. Adams was out at a construction site, the impersonal voice said, and not expected back at the office today. Would I like to leave a message? I was tempted, but didn't. So I hung up and sat there contemplating my navel for a while. Then the phone rang.

"Boyd," I said briskly, because maybe it was a client, and as I had just lost a client, I was in need of a new client.

"Danny!" The voice sounded desperate.

"Eleanor?"

"They said to tell you that you've got twenty-four hours to leave Santo Bahia," she said. "If you don't, they'll kill me."

"Let me talk with one of them," I said quickly.

There was silence, like somebody had put his hands over the mouthpiece, which lasted for around ten seconds.

"They won't talk with you, Danny," she said, and her voice sounded very tired. "They say that's it. Either you leave within the next twenty-four hours, or they'll kill me."

"Are you all right?"

"I guess so. Good-bye, Danny." There was a faint click as she hung up.

I went back into my two-room complex, lifted the Magnum and the shoulder rig out of the bureau drawer, and put them on. Then I went down to the car and drove out to the cottage at Paradise Beach. Melanie opened the door with a glass in her hand and had a little problem there bringing me into focus.

"Too late for lunch," she said, and her voice was slightly slurred, "and I told you before, I hate sex in the afternoons."

"First thing in the morning, you said," I reminded her.

"The afternoons, too," she said. "I'm a very choosy kind of lady, Danny Boyd, so scram!"

"How many martinis have you drunk since I left?"

She smiled vaguely. "Who's counting?"

I put my hand against the swell of her right breast and pushed gently. She backed off inside the cottage, and I kicked the door shut behind me. Then I lifted the glass out of her hand.

"I told you," she said thickly, "no sex in the after- noons!"

"We have to go visiting," I said.

"I'm not going any place!" she said firmly. "I was just thinking, when I've finished my drink I'm going to lie down and have a little nap."

"Wrong," I said.

"Wrong?"

"Definitely wrong!"

I put the glass down on the bartop, put my hand back against the firm swell of her right breast, and pushed again. She went backward obediently and frowned as she tried to concentrate.

"Where are we going, Danny?"

"The bathroom," I said.

"I don't want to go to the bathroom!"

"Don't fight it," I said. "This thing is bigger than the both of us."

When we got inside the bathroom, I took my hand away and looked at her. Her eyes made another big effort and brought me into focus again. She was also swaying a little on her feet.

"Hold your hands above your head," I told her.

"What for?"

"Just do it!"

So she held her arms up above her head, and I peeled off the cotton top briskly.

"Danny!" She shook her head slowly. "I told you, I hate sex in the afternoons."

I unzipped her shorts and pulled them down around her ankles. She made a protesting sound, took a step forward, and tripped over her shorts. I caught her before she smashed her head on the tiled floor, stripped the shorts from around her ankles, and pushed her into the shower stall.

"It's rape," she said thickly. "I'll tell Captain Schell, you see if I don't!"

I turned her around so her back was toward me. I gave her high rounded buttocks a resounding slap for good measure, then getting a good grip on her hair, turned the faucet full on. She screeched as the cold water cascaded all over her, and wriggled violently, but I kept a real tight grip on her hair so she had no way of escaping it. I held her there for a good five minutes before I turned off the faucet.

"You bastard!" she said with great feeling. "I would have preferred rape."

I tossed a bath towel at her, then went out to the kitchen and made some strong coffee. When I got back to the bathroom, she was sitting on the toilet seat, gazing bleakly into the middle distance. Her thighs were pressed together, showing only a narrow wedge of her pubis.

"Drink this," I told her, and handed her the cup of coffee.

"I've just come to a decision," she said. "You must

78

really like me, Danny, or you wouldn't go to all this bother, right?"

"You're my client," I said.

"Don't you think that's just a little cold-blooded?" she said. "I mean, I bet you don't go to all this trouble for just any little old client, right? You can rape me now if you want, I won't mind. Or a nice, quick, clean blow-job if you don't want to go to too much trouble." She swallowed a mouthful of coffee, and sighed gently. "I could like it, even, and don't tell me it's afternoon because I don't want to know."

"Finish your coffee," I said, "dry your hair. Then put some pretty clothes on, because we're going visiting."

"Visiting?" Her violet eyes looked mildly interested. "Who with?"

"Bobo Shanks," I said. "He's going to tell us all about his orgies."

She gulped down some more coffee then looked up at me again. "Okay," she said. "I know what you're trying to do to me, Danny. You're just trying to embarrass me so I'll tell you about the orgies, right?"

It was one hell of a moment for the doorbell to ring. Her eyes widened as she heard it.

"You better go find out who it is, Danny," she said wisely, "because if you don't, you'll never know, right?"

So I went and opened the front door. Standing there was a big bull of a guy, bald on top, with bright red hair around the edges. He was wearing a checked shirt and tartan pants, and the blue eyes, too close together, bulged when he saw me.

"Christ!" he bellowed. "You!"

"Hi, Hy," I said wittily.

"I'll take you apart," he said happily. "Tear off your

arms and stuff them down your throat. And then I'm going to tear off your legs and stuff them up your ass! Then I'm going to get me a mallet and hammer you down for a marking peg out on the site!"

It was no time to play games and, besides, my head was starting to throb again. So I pulled the Magnum out of the shoulder rig and pushed the barrel into his stomach.

"Cool it," I told him.

"Fuck you!" he said, but his heart wasn't in it.

"I'll get around to you," I promised him, "but your time isn't yet."

"What the hell are you talking about?"

"For now," I said, "go away. Get lost. Go play developer someplace else."

"You're crazy!" he said.

"I pull the trigger and you're dead."

He thought about it and didn't like the implications. So he backed off carefully, and then, when he was about six feet away from the front door, suddenly got brave.

"I'll be back, Boyd," he said.

Just to one side of him was parked this beautiful gold and white Cadillac Eldorado.

"Is that your car?" I asked him.

"Goddamned right it's my car," he said. "What the hell—"

I depressed the barrel of the Magnum and pulled the trigger. The gas tank was a big enough target and a sudden jet of gas erupted through the bullet hole.

"Wherever you're going," I said, "you want to get there fast before you run out of gas."

"Why, you—!"

I depressed the barrel of the Magnum another inch

and pulled the trigger again. Dust spurted between his feet. He let out a startled yelp and got into the car real fast. I watched him drive away with his back wheels spraying dust, and felt a momentary warm glow inside. Then I closed the front door and went back to the bathroom. Melanie was still sitting on the toilet seat, drinking her coffee.

"Who was it?" she asked.

"Some guy selling second-hand automobiles," I said.

"I don't know about the orgies," she said. "They were only rumors."

"Rumors?"

"Bobo and Sarah used to kind of hint at them," she said, "but I never paid much mind. I figured they were just trying to get at me, you know?"

"No," I said. "Tell me."

"They'd talk about the swinging time they'd had the previous night and how I'd missed out again," she said. "I figured they were only kidding, trying to get a big rise out of me."

"So you don't know if the orgies were for real?"

She sighed heavily. "That's what I keep on trying to tell you right?"

"Okay," I said. "Now dry your hair and put on some clothes."

"He'll kill you, Danny," she said soberly. "After what you did to him last night."

"Shanks?"

"Either him or Hy Adams," she said, "or maybe the both of them. And if they don't, Sarah sure as hell will kill you after you hacked her shin that way."

"One of them killed Broderick," I said. "Maybe all three of them. Who the hell else?"

"I'm not going with you!" Her face set in a tight

mold. "No way, Danny. I'm not getting involved. Besides, what the hell did I hire you for and pay you all that good money?"

I figured, reluctantly, she had a point.

Chapter Eight

Captain Schell wasn't exactly enchanted to see me. He lighted a thin black cigar, blew a cloud of smoke toward the ceiling, then finally deigned to look in my direction.

"I'm a busy man, Boyd," he said. "So make it brief. Whatever it is you want, the answer is no."

"Anything interesting in the autopsy result?"

"No," he said flatly. "Somebody used the serrated knife to cut his throat, exactly the way it looked. Surprise, surprise!"

"Any other leads?"

"None."

"Adams Constructions, Inc., is owned by Hy Adams," I said.

"You're absolutely right."

"What do you know about him?"

"He's a very successful man, operating a strictly legitimate enterprise."

"With a taste for private orgies on the side," I said.

"News to me," he grunted.

"The orgies are staged by Bobo Shanks," I said, "who has a nasty reputation for sadism on the side. A maid who needed emergency surgery in the middle of the night, for example. Then there was the tourist he nearly killed in a bar one night."

"I don't know where you get your information but it's inaccurate," he said. "I never heard of any maid, and the tourist started the fight in the bar. There were a half-dozen eyewitnesses to prove it."

"What *do* you know about Shanks?"

"He's a man of considerable private means, comes from one of the oldest Santo Bahia families, and has a blameless reputation," he said. "And before you ask, Charles Gray is a very respectable attorney-at-law, period! I also can't see any possible motive for Sarah Rigby wanting to kill her brother. But I can see a very strong motive for Melanie Rigby wanting to kill her husband. Only you say she didn't because you were with her at the time. I'm working on it, Boyd."

"How about the will?" I asked him.

"I had to twist Gray's arm a little there," he said. "The estate should be worth around a million dollars. One-third goes to the wife, and the rest goes to any surviving members of the family. That means two-thirds goes to the sister."

"And it gives her double the motive it gives his wife," I said. "She figured on going for a settlement of around four hundred thousand, anyway."

"Did she?" He shuffled the papers on his desk. "Good-bye, Boyd."

"Thanks for nothing, Captain," I said.

He let me reach the doorway before he spoke again.

"I'm just a hick cop," he said. "By the time I heard about the maid it was a couple of days after she had left town. And the surgery was done in a very exclusive private hospital that would close down tomorrow if it wasn't supported by the old monied families we have around here."

"Is that right?" I said in a neutral voice.

"If you start creating a little hell with these rich, important families around here," he said mildly, "I warn you now, Boyd, they'll expect action from me and they'll get it."

"Sure," I said. "I understand."

"Of course," he continued, in an even milder voice, "if you do decide to raise a little hell there's not much I can do to stop you."

"Thank you," I said. "Good-bye, Captain."

"Good-bye, Boyd," he said, and started shuffling through his papers again.

I went back to the office, and by the time I got there it was late afternoon. It was the time I usually went to the beach but it seemed wrong somehow to go and sprawl out on the sand while the kidnappers were still holding poor Eleanor. So I stayed right where I was, and the phone rang around ten minutes later.

"Boyd?" a bull-like voice roared in my ear.

"Boyd," I agreed.

"This is Hy Adams here. Look! The easiest thing for me to do right now would be to come over there and beat your brains to a pulp. But I'm confused. Why?"

"You're asking me why you're confused?"

"I'm asking why you beat the hell out of me the other night when I wasn't looking," he said. "Then, this afternoon, you pulled a gun on me and—" he almost choked on the memory "—put a goddamned hole in the gas tank of my new car. Why, for Christ's sake?"

"A kind of defensive reflex, I guess," I said. "You come on so strong all the time."

"There's got to be a better reason, Boyd. Melanie hired you to find out who murdered her husband, right?"

"Right," I agreed.

"So why the hell aren't you busy finding out for her?" he said. "I mean, instead of conducting this personal vendetta against me the whole goddamned time!"

"I figure you're involved," I said. "Not directly, I mean, but involved with the people who killed her husband."

"And just who the hell did kill her husband?"

"Sarah Rigby and Bobo Shanks," I said easily.

"Are you crazy?" he bellowed.

"They're capable of it," I said. "Just because they turned on a couple of good orgies for you from time to time doesn't mean they're nice people, Hy."

"Orgies?" he almost screamed. "What the hell orgies are you babbling about?"

"How much money have they got invested in your developments right now?" I said.

"You're crazy, Boyd," he said tightly. "You have to be out of your mind."

"How much?"

"None of your goddamned business," he roared. "And if you mess with me again, I'll kill you. That's a promise!"

He hung up by slamming down the phone in my ear. I went and made myself a drink, and brought it back to the phone. Then I dialed the number of the Paradise Beach cottage. Melanie answered on the second ring.

"How are you feeling, nice and sober?" I asked brightly.

"I'm feeling dreadful," she said. "I was just about to start drinking again, and this time I'm not about to stop until I keel over."

"His estate is worth around a million," I said.

"Broderick's estate?" her voice brightened. "Did you find out how much he left me, Danny?"

"A third," I said, "the other two-thirds goes to any surviving relatives—excluding you, of course—and that means dear Sarah gets two-thirds."

"The bitch!" she said coldly.

"I just talked with Hy Adams," I said. "He wants to know why I don't like him, and I told him he was involved in the orgies Bobo Shanks throws in his house. Hy didn't like it at all."

"I don't blame him," she said.

"But there were orgies, right?"

"I told you before, Sarah and Bobo hinted at them, that's all," she said coldly.

"How about Broderick?"

"He never mentioned anything about them," she said. "I'm sure they were fantasies dreamed up by Sarah and Bobo to try and make me feel upset."

"I'd still like you to visit with me tonight," I said.

"Where?" Her voice was very cautious.

"Shanks' place."

"No chance," she said coldly. "You're the one who's getting paid to take the risks, Danny, not me!"

Then it was her turn to hang up. Everybody got to hang up first but me. I retreated to my two-room complex, had a shower, then got dressed again and made myself another drink. Then I wondered where and what I'd eat for dinner. Chicken and pancakes were definitely out. The phone rang again and I wondered if I should answer, then hang up real fast.

"Mr. Boyd?" The voice was cool and arrogant.

"Miss Rigby," I said. "How's the shinbone?"

"I thought it was quite amusing," she said. "In retrospect, of course. Are you free for dinner tonight?"

"Sure," I said.

"You might care to have dinner at my house," she said, "around eight?"

"It sounds fine," I said. "Just the two of us?"

"Just the three of us," she said. "Bobo is coming, too."

"I hope he figures it was quite amusing," I said, "in retrospect, of course."

"I expect we'll find out," she said. "Or does the thought make you feel nervous, Mr. Boyd?"

"Just cautious," I said. "I'll see you around eight, Miss Rigby." Then I hung up real fast because I didn't want to be a third-time loser.

The thing was, I asked myself a couple of hours later, did the well-dressed dinner guest wear a shoulder rig? I figured the answer was an affirmative, then put my coat back on over it. The rig was custommade, so there was no bulge. I went down to the car and wondered just what the hell I was doing. The obvious answer was that I was being a catalyst, and that has a nice ring to it of derring-do and save six for pallbearers. Closer to the truth, I figured as I pushed the car gently down the main drag, was the simple fact that I was desperate. The only people who could give me a lead just were not talking, so maybe if I pushed them hard enough they would start talking. Either that, or they might put a bullet through the back of my head. Anyway, I guessed deduction was the privilege of the professional cop, and the only way the private cop could stay in business was by taking his lumps. And I was owed quite a lot of lumps already, I remembered sourly.

It was five after eight when I arrived at the Rigby residence up on Sublime Point. The chimes played inside the house and then the front door opened a few seconds later. Her sleek black hair was brushed tight against the sides of her head from a center part, her fine-chiseled features had their natural haughty look, and her dark eyes fixed me with a steady, unblinking gaze. She was wearing another white dress but this one was made from a thin silk that clung to her figure with a kind of loving care. The low scalloped neckline just cleared the nipple-line of her small, high breasts with a fraction of an inch to spare. She looked sexy, and deadly, and the twist to her mouth was purely sensual.

"How nice of you to be prompt, Mr. Boyd," she said.

"The invitation was irresistible," I told her.

"Why don't you come in." She opened the door wider with a flourish.

I followed her into the living room, and found Shanks already established in an armchair. He looked about the same with his long blond hair and matching mustache, but I saw with a strong feeling of satisfaction that his nose was red and swollen. His bright blue eyes gave me an indifferent acknowledgement, then he looked away.

"We are very generous people here in Santo Bahia," Sarah Rigby said. "Everything is forgiven and forgotten, Mr. Boyd. Isn't that right, Bobo?"

Shanks bared his pearly-white teeth at me in brief grimace. "Just don't ever try anything like that again,

89

Boyd," he said. "The next time I'll be ready and waiting."

"Bourbon on the rocks, as I remember," Sarah said. "Correct, Mr. Boyd?"

"Right on," I said.

She made the drink and handed it to me, then walked across to the nearest chair and sat down. The both of them were silent, watching me drink my drink like I was some kind of a rare zoological specimen.

"And how is your investigation progressing, Mr. Boyd?" Sarah asked finally.

"Slowly," I said. "Maybe you can help. When you and Bobo, here, were talking about orgies to Melanie, were you for real or only kidding?"

"Orgies?" Shanks said.

"Sexual orgies," I said helpfully. "The word around town is you're a sadist, Bobo. There was this housemaid of yours who needed surgery in the middle of the night after one of your orgies. Then there was this tourist you nearly killed in a bar brawl one night. But orgies are your specialty, I hear. You even have the girls brought in from out of town."

"We've always had sexual orgies here in Santo Bahia, Mr. Boyd," Sarah said. "All the best families do. It's *de rigueur*, if you understand my meaning."

"It's rigid?"

"It was my fault, Mr. Boyd," she said apologetically. "For a moment there, I forgot you were a cretin."

"I guess an orgy here and there impresses the local business community," I said. "Guys like Hy Adams, for example."

"For example," she said. "Bobo even has a room especially equipped for orgies. Isn't that right, Bobo?"

"Sure," he said idly, "from whippy little canes to big black dildos. You name it, and I've got it."

"Perhaps you may care to see it for yourself later, Mr. Boyd," Sarah said. "After dinner?"

"It sounds fascinating, Miss Rigby," I said.

"What do you think it will prove?" She smiled at me lazily. "Bobo's special orgy room, I mean."

"I wouldn't know," I told her.

"He's being modest," Shanks said, "or maybe he really is just a man of action. Like he can only get results by beating the hell out of people." He grinned suddenly. "I can sympathize with him. It's not a bad philosophy."

"He's a very good-looking man," Sarah said, "and he knows it, of course. Vanity is his middle name."

"If he performs as well as he looks it could be a formidable combination," Shanks said.

"And only Melanie can tell us for sure. What a shame she isn't here right now to confide her girlish secrets." Sarah smiled at me again. "I did invite her, you know, but she declined."

"How about Adams," I said. "Did you invite him?"

She shook her head. "It just wouldn't be his kind of an evening. Hy is a delightful person but still crude around the edges. Isn't that right, Bobo?"

"Absolutely," Shanks said. "A charming man, but definitely crude about the edges."

"How's your drink, Mr. Boyd?" Sarah asked.

"Just fine," I told her.

"Drink up," she said, "you'll have time for another one before dinner." She smiled at me yet again. "You're a fun person, Mr. Boyd, did you know that?"

I stared at her. "A fun person?"

"So dynamic, and so physical," she said. "So gallant in defending devious little Melanie, who made my

91

poor brother's life hell on wheels! And how can I ever forget the last time you were here and the charming insinuation you made then? The one about my having an incestuous relationship with my brother when he was alive. Then the way you savagely beat up poor Bobo here. I did so admire the way you never gave him a chance to get up out of his chair before you attacked him. And your gentlemanly instincts, Mr. Boyd! The way you viciously hacked my shinbone had me lost in admiration. I'm still carrying the most dreadful bruise!"

I finished my drink while I tried to think up an answer to that. She got up out of her chair and took the glass out of my hand.

"I don't think you'll need another drink, Mr. Boyd," she said briskly. "One of my specials will be quite enough for you."

"You gave it to him before dinner?" Shanks sounded mildly surprised.

"I'm sure he'll perform a lot better on an empty stomach," she said.

"What the hell are you talking about?" I asked.

She turned toward me and the smile on her face expanded until it stretched from ear to ear.

"Don't do that," I told her. "It unnerves me."

"We owe you a debt, Mr. Boyd," she said. "Or, to be strictly accurate, you owe us a debt. And tonight you're going to get your chance to repay it."

The ear-to-ear grin suddenly slipped, and now her whole neck was one dreadful expanse of shiny white teeth.

"Your grin slipped," I said.

"How's that, Mr. Boyd?"

"Your grin has slipped," I said very carefully. "Please put it back up onto your face."

"Speak up, Mr. Boyd," she said tartly. "We can hardly hear you at all."

"Your grin—" I stopped right there because her whole face wavered, then started to dissolve. "It's goddamned hot in here," I said feebly.

"He's a long time going," Shanks said. "Are you sure you haven't been diluting that stuff?"

"You don't feel too good, Mr. Boyd?" Sarah's voice sounded as if it came from a great distance. "Don't worry, it's nothing permanent. Just a little something I put into your drink. It will only last about a half hour."

A dark cloud slowly enveloped me and I frantically grabbed for the arms of the chair.

"You want to catch him as he falls, Bobo?" I heard her voice ask, from somewhere inside the black cloud. "No? Oh, well, I don't suppose it matters."

Chapter Nine

I opened my eyes and the room swam slowly into focus. There was this one bright light shining directly down on me, and the rest of the room was full of shadows. My arms ached like hell.

"Feeling better now, Mr. Boyd?" Sarah's voice asked from someplace deep in the shadows.

I was standing upright, I realized, or sagging upright, with my arms tied above my head. So I braced myself on my feet and it eased my aching arms a little. When I looked down at myself, I saw I wasn't wearing any clothes.

"Just what the hell was it you gave me in the drink?" I muttered.

"Something I find very effective. No after effects, either, you'll be glad to hear. You should be feeling your usual virile self at any moment now, Mr. Boyd."

She moved into the narrow circle of light and came toward me at a slow pace. She was completely naked.

Stripped, her body was startlingly feminine; her small breasts had large erect nipples, and there was a surprisingly thick thatch of lush curly black hair between the tops of her thighs, clustered thickly along the edges of her slightly parted slit. She placed both her hands on my chest, then drew them slowly down the length of my body. They hovered over my chest and stomach, and her fingers rustled against my pubic hair.

"Perhaps I should have said I'm feeling your usual virile self." She chuckled briefly as one hand closed over my shaft. "This is the orgy room, Mr. Boyd." Her fingers stroked me with a deft touch and I felt my shaft begin to stiffen. "That's better, Mr. Boyd."

Her hand continued the expert stroking until my shaft was fiercely erect. Then her other hand encircled my testicles and squeezed them hard. I grunted painfully, and she chuckled again.

"I'm so glad I have your complete attention, Mr. Boyd," she said, then squeezed again, even harder.

I bit down hard on my lower lip and felt the sweat beading my forehead. Then she relaxed her grip with both hands and moved away from me, a faint smile still on her face.

"I almost forgot, Mr. Boyd," she said. "You're the grand finale, not the hors d'oeuvre!"

The light swiveled away from me across the room, lighting up another figure who was lashed the same way as I was to a steel X-frame. Her dark brown hair hung loosely around her shoulders and her eyes were closed. Her body was real familiar, with the thrusting full breasts, soft curve to the belly, and the taut thighs.

"Say hello to Mr. Boyd, dear," Sarah said brightly.

Eleanor Townsend said nothing and kept her eyes tightly closed. Bobo Shanks emerged from the shadows into the light, also naked. His whole body was a light golden color and he looked like a walking commercial for somebody's suntan oil. His thick, powerful log was semi-erect—or that may have been its usual supine condition.

"Naughty, Eleanor," he said in a reproachful voice. "Now you say hello to Mr. Boyd, you hear?"

His hand cupped her right breast for a moment, then squeezed it viciously. Eleanor gasped with the pain and opened her eyes.

"Hello, Danny," she whispered.

"Not exactly a touching reunion," Sarah said. "Perhaps you're disappointed at his still being here in Santo Bahia, Eleanor. After all, you told him yourself if he didn't leave inside twenty-four hours you were going to be killed. And he's still here!"

"I figured I'd find her anyway," I said.

"And you surely did," Shanks said. "Who'd have guessed it, Boyd? I mean all this—" he cupped both of Eleanor's breasts in his hands and lifted them slightly "—was lurking under those dreadful clothes she always wears!"

"All right, Bobo," Sarah said coldly. "She's here to be punished, remember, not fondled by your hot little hands!"

"Punished," I said, "for what?"

"She was altogether too friendly toward you," Sarah said in a prim-sounding voice. "Far too friendly. She even went to bed with you, Boyd!"

Shanks turned away with a sullen look on his face and untied Eleanor's wrists and ankles. Then he made her turn around, and lashed her back onto the steel triangle. Beneath her buttocks, a tuft of dark hair showed between her parted legs.

"Perhaps it wasn't her fault?" Sarah said idly. "She just couldn't resist your good looks and virility, Mr. Boyd. Is that it, do you think?"

I watched as Shanks vanished into the shadows,

then reappeared carrying a small whip which had maybe a half-dozen leather thongs, all of which were lead-tipped.

"A kind of miniature version of the cat-o-nine-tails," Shanks said in a jovial voice. "It hurts like hell!"

He raised his arm and brought the whip down across Eleanor's rounded bottom. She screamed as the lead tips bit into her flesh and drew blood. Then she screamed again and again as he whipped her with an ever-increasing ferocity until her body suddenly sagged limply, supported by her bound wrists. Blood dripped from the cuts in her flesh and trickled down the backs of her thighs.

"Hey!" Shanks exhaled sharply. "I enjoyed that. Doesn't leave any permanent scars, you know."

"Take her down," Sarah said. "She's had enough for now."

"Take her down?" Shanks said in a disbelieving voice. "But I've only just started!"

"You've finished for now," she said. "There'll be plenty of time later to indulge yourself with her. Right now I'm concerned with Mr. Boyd."

"Oh!" Shanks nodded his head understandingly. "Is there anything I can do to help?"

"Not a thing," she said. "Just get the Townsend woman out of here and leave me alone for a while."

Shanks untied Eleanor's hands and feet, slung her limp body over his shoulder, and carried her back into the shadows. I heard the sound of a door closing a few seconds later.

"A couple of things first, Mr. Boyd," Sarah said. "If you told anybody about the things that have happened here tonight they wouldn't believe you. And we're going to keep Eleanor around. But not in this house, or my house, either. Someplace where she'll be completely safe until you've left Santo Bahia for good. We won't kill her." She smiled broadly. "You can be assured of that, Mr. Boyd. But for every twenty-four hours you remain in Santo Bahia, she'll get another beating like the one you just saw. Only each successive time the beating will be worse. I'm sure Bobo is hoping you'll stay a long while. You can see how enthusiastic he is."

"You're crazy," I said, "the both of you. Was your brother crazy, too?"

She backhanded me across the mouth. "Don't you dare mention my brother's name," she hissed at me. "Not with your dirty mouth!"

"Okay," I said. "What happens now?"

"I don't want to hurry it," she said. "I want the both of us to enjoy every second of it."

She came closer, one hand seizing my shaft again and gently stroking it. As she did so, she leaned the top half of her body forward so her small breasts pushed against my chest. Then she moved her shoulders slowly so her taut nipples rubbed hard against my skin. My shaft came erect and she made small murmuring sounds of approval. A few seconds later she came up on tiptoe, then pushed my shaft between her legs. Her hands gripped hard on my shoulders and her nails dug deep as she kept up a slow, continuous movement, her slit pressing down hard onto my throbbing shaft. She groaned a couple of times and her eyes closed. I could feel the growing moistness and softness as she pressed down even harder, and then she suddenly grunted and her whole body shuddered convulsively. For a long moment her body lay limp against mine, and then her eyes opened again. She pushed herself away from me, a look of revulsion on her face, then grabbed hold of my testicles and squeezed them viciously.

"You dirty bastard!" she said thickly. "You'd like to try and get inside me, wouldn't you? Well, no man ever has, and no man ever will, you hear?"

Then she let go suddenly, walked across the room quickly, and picked up the bloodstained whip Shanks had dropped on the floor.

"I'll teach you to point that filthy thing at me!"

The whip flailed through the air and I screamed when it connected, because I just couldn't help it. The pain was unbelievable, and it felt like my genitals had been torn apart. She raised the whip a second time, then flailed it down across my stomach, and then a third time across my chest. I had stopped screaming then because I was too busy biting through my lower lip. She moved around behind me and started using the whip on my back, working her way down from my shoulders without hurrying. Somewhere along the line I passed out cold.

When I woke up I was fully dressed and in the front seat of my own car. My whole body felt like it was on fire, and when I sat up I could feel the shirt sticking to my back. I looked out the windshield and realized I didn't have to worry about getting home because I was there already, parked right out front. My head felt dizzy when I moved, and it took me a hell of a long time to get out of the car and up to the apartment. I walked slowly, like a little old man, through to the bedroom and started the shower running. My watch said it was twenty minutes after midnight. I took it off, then slowly peeled off my coat. Everything was there—the gun in the shoulder rig, the wallet in the inside pocket. I got rid of the gun and the rig. It took a while to get off my shoes and socks, because bending didn't help any. Then I got rid of my pants. The shorts and the shirt were stuck to me. So I stood under the shower and winced as the cold water hit me, then managed to get rid of the rest of my clothes when they had become saturated. Afterward I patted myself dry with a bath towel, then took a look in the mirror. It wasn't a reassuring sight. I looked like I had just been run through an automatic harvester. But nothing seemed to be missing and that was something to be thankful for.

I walked slowly out in to the living room and made myself a drink. If Sarah could doctor my drink, I guessed she could have plunged a needle into my arm after I had fainted, and that would account for me waking up fully dressed in my own car, parked outside my own office and apartment. I found a salve and gingerly applied it to all the cuts I could reach. A very careful scrutiny of my vital parts was reassuring. Cut and battered it might be, but it looked as if my shaft would live to rise another day. I drank my drink while I brooded, then made another drink while I brooded some more. Halfway through the second drink I picked up the phone and dialed Sarah Rigby's number. It rang for a long time before she answered.

"Who the hell is this?" she almost snarled. "It's the middle of the goddamned night!"

"Boyd," I said.

"Boyd?" Her voice was suddenly wide awake. "What is it, Mr. Boyd? You've just discovered you like it and you want to come back for some more?"

"If I leave Santo Bahia," I said, "what happens to Eleanor Townsend?"

"I won't let Bobo get near her with his nasty little whip, if that's what you mean," she said. "I promise you."

"You mean you're going to keep her a prisoner someplace for the rest of her life?"

"There's no need for that," she said. "Eleanor's learned her lesson already. When we're sure you've left Santo Bahia for good, Mr. Boyd, we'll let her go."

"How long will it take to convince you I've gone for good?"

"Who knows?" she said. "A week, maybe two weeks."

"Okay," I said. "You've got yourself a deal."

"Are you hurting much right now, Mr. Boyd?" She couldn't quite keep the gloating tone out of her voice. "All over, and the tender parts especially?"

"I was disappointed in you, Sarah," I said. "Your lovemaking is lousy. I mean, no penetration."

"If any man ever thinks he's going to stick his filthy thing into me—"

"I've been thinking about it," I said. "It's a real big hang-up with you, Sarah. No penetration. If there's no penetration, you could almost kid yourself you weren't doing what you were actually doing, right?"

"I don't know what you're talking about," she hissed, "and I don't want to know!"

"If you were doing something you knew was bad, but then you didn't really do it because there was no penetration, it wouldn't seem so bad," I said. "It probably started when you were both in your teens, I guess, and starting to grow up. That's when we get all our real big sexual hang-ups, the shrinks say."

"I still don't know what you're talking about!"

"Okay," I said. "I'm sorry I'm boring you. Why don't you just hang up on me, Sarah, and go right back to sleep?"

"Tell me!" She almost screamed the words down the phone.

"Goddamn you, Boyd. Tell me!"

"It's very obvious when you think about it," I said. "I mean, that's how you and Broderick got started, right? But with no penetration, you could kid yourselves you weren't really doing it at all. So it was brother and sister just having a little private fun, and incest never came into it."

She made a harsh grunting sound in my ear like a wounded animal at bay, then hung up. I finished my drink, made myself a third, then picked up the phone again and dialed the number of the Paradise Beach cottage. The phone rang and rang, but I was patient because I had nothing else exciting to do. Then finally somebody lifted it off the hook.

"*What!*" Melanie screamed in my ear.

"Let me talk with Hy," I said briskly.

"*What?*"

"Let me talk with Hy," I repeated in a brisk voice. "I guess if you move one of your beautiful breasts out of the way, he'll be able to reach the phone with no trouble at all."

"Oh, my God!" she said. "You just don't have any idea what he's got to move out of the way before he can talk with you."

There was a kind of dead silence while she held her hand over the phone, I presumed, then Adams' voice bellowed in my ear.

"This does it up just fine, Boyd!" he yelled. "First thing in the morning, I'm going to kill you!"

"Make it lunchtime," I said. "There's a little restaurant on a bay along the coast. Melanie can tell you the name of it. I'll meet you there around one."

"What for?" he said. "So you can set fire to me, or something?"

"We should talk," I said. "It's important."

"Tell me something," he said, "do you mind me screwing Melanie? I mean, do you have some deep-rooted objection?"

"No," I said.

"It happens every time," he said in a wondering voice. "I've just got it in and then—bam!—along comes Boyd!"

"I'm sorry about the interruption," I said. "I'll see you for lunch then, okay?"

"What can I lose?" he said. "Okay—Melanie, my new Cadillac, my life, probably. So I'll live dangerously, Boyd."

"And don't you dare try and call back," Melanie's voice said a moment later. "Because I'm leaving the phone off the hook, you hear, Danny Boyd!"

"While you're about it, you should take Hy Adams off the hook, too," I told her, then hung up.

Chapter Ten

∿∿∿∿∿∿∿∿∿∿∿∿∿∿∿∿∿∿∿∿∿∿∿∿∿∿∿∿∿∿∿∿

I was sitting there in the sun on the balcony, drinking my martini, and trying real hard to feel suave and sophisticated with the shirt sticking to my painful back, when Hy Adams arrived. He came bouncing up to the table, wearing a wild-patterned Hawaiian shirt and blue pants. The thick red mustache was kind of waffling in the breeze, and his bald pate had a kind of bronzed glow to it from the reflected sunlight. He pulled out a chair when he reached the table and sat down heavily. The light blue eyes were bright with suspicion as he glared at me.

"Okay, Boyd," he said. "Where is it?"

"What?"

"Whatever the hell it is you've mickey-moused, that's what!" he looked around quickly. "The chair, huh? Maybe that's it. You've wired a bomb to the underside, right?"

"Relax," I told him. "What are you drinking?"

"Rye," he said, "on the rocks. And I want you should taste it first, Boyd!"

"I went to an orgy at Bobo Shanks' house last night," I said.

"You—what?"

I figured it would hold him for a while, and it did. The waiter homed in on the table and I ordered Adams' drink. And all the while Adams waited expectantly, his mustache waffling with maybe a little more than the breeze. I smiled vaguely at him and waited until his drink was delivered.

"Okay," Adams said thickly. "So tell me about the orgy!"

"What's to tell?" I said. "You've been to a few, right?"

He took a deep swallow of rye on the rocks, then wiped his mustache carefully with his pocket handkerchief.

"Okay," he said in a resigned voice. "It was a come-on. I don't come on to a come-on, Boyd."

"They're sick," I said, "the both of them."

"You're just out of New York, right?" he said. "It's different from the rest of the United States, they tell me. Okay, I'll believe it. So, back there in Manhattan, maybe everybody knows exactly what you're talking about, Boyd, because they're real smart. But out here on the West Coast we're just a bunch of plain simple people who upped out of Oregon and Ioway, and all those Midwest states. But our roots are still back there. So you just have to spell things out for me, Boyd. Like who is the both of them who is sick?"

I shook my head admiringly. "Is that how you took all them real eddificated folk who live up on the hill when you first came here, Hy?"

He grinned cautiously. "Some of them like it, you'd be surprised. You have to be real careful you don't push it too far. I don't say 'Shucks!' anymore, or chew on grass. First couple of months it went real well, but then they started getting suspicious when they found out I'd screwed them on a couple of the best tracts that were just lying around here waiting to be developed. So I got me a new image. Shrewd, but still real impressed by the gentlefolk."

"Especially when they invited you to their orgies?"

"Now you just gone and done it again, boy." He grinned slowly. "Why don't you quit being cute, Boyd, and tell me what it is you want to know."

"What was Broderick Rigby like?" I said.

He shrugged. "I never knew him that well. Sure, he was around a lot, but Sarah was always the brains of the family so I did most all of my talking to her. He never seemed bothered about the business end of things."

"The Rigby family invested with you," I said. "That new motel and canal complex, for example?"

"That's right," he said. "They owned a swamp, and I needed that swamp. I also needed development capital. They had that, too. So I went and talked with their stiff-dicked attorney."

"Charles Gray?" I said.

"The same." He nodded slowly. "They dickered for a while. Figured they could sell their swamp to some other developer and not have to worry about investment. I told them I could get another investor to buy it from them, and then develop it. It was me doing them a favor, I said. Finally they saw it my way around."

"How much money did they put up?"

"They put up their swamp, and one-million-five," he said. "I put up my know-how, my construction company, and three hundred thousand. It's a good deal for everybody all the way around."

"There's no chance of anybody losing money?"

"There's always a chance of everybody losing everything," he said. "But this one looks real good."

"Suppose somebody wanted to take out their money in a hurry?" I said.

"No way," he said flatly. "All that money is sunk into expertise and concrete and timber and plumbing, and you name it. And nothing's finished right now. This is the one stage in a development project where you can't pull out. If you try, some lousy little bank will come sniffing around finally and offer you ten cents on the dollar for the uncompleted project. You get screwed and tattooed in a situation like that, Boyd, but you never get wooed first!"

"Broderick's estate should be worth a million before taxes, I hear," I said.

"When the motel and canal complex has paid off a couple of years from now, then maybe," he said. "But not before, Boyd. My guess is that million-five cleaned out just about what real money the Rigbys had."

"So Melanie and Sarah Rigby are going to have to wait for their money after probate?" I said.

"They surely are." He grinned happily.

"If he'd lived and gotten the divorce," I said, "Melanie would have still had to wait for her settlement the same way, right?"

"I guess so," he said. "What the hell else?"

"You want another drink?"

He settled back in his chair comfortably. "I always want another drink, Boyd."

I flagged down the waiter, then looked at him again. "You and Melanie were screwing while she was still married, she told me."

"Is that the delicate way you New York sophisticates put it?" He chuckled suddenly. "Yeah, sure we were. She wasn't getting much from Broderick and she's the kind of girl who needs to get it regular."

The waiter served the drinks and I asked Adams if he'd like to order lunch.

"Why not?" he said. "Tell the chef I'll have my usual."

"Yes, sir, Mr. Adams," the waiter said, then gave me an inquiring look.

"I'll have Mr. Adams' usual, too," I said. "Whatever the hell that is." I watched the waiter depart, then looked at Adams. "Is this how you simple country boys do it?"

"I eat here a couple of days a week, on average," he said comfortably. "If you want an honest opinion, Boyd, I figure Broderick always had trouble getting it up for anybody except his sister."

"You know for sure?"

"Nah!" He shook his head firmly. "Just a kind of educated guess is all."

"So why would he marry Melanie?"

"Maybe he wanted to kick the habit?" Adams lifted his thick eyebrows suddenly. "He wouldn't be the first guy to try and kick a bad habit, then fail, right?"

"I guess not," I said.

"I figure Sarah saw what I was thinking, because, suddenly, I was invited to this big private orgy out at Shanks' house," he said. "It was okay, I guess. The girls he brought in from out of town were real high class hookers. But then they started getting into some real kinky routines and it turned me right off. I like to screw, you know. Maybe it makes me one of the old-fashioned guys, but that's what I like to do. Whipping some broad's bare ass with a bunch of feathers isn't my idea of having fun."

"With a bunch of feathers?" I said incredulously.

"Well, it only happened just the one time," he admitted. "Most other times they used real canes and whips, and don't ask me what else!"

"Who was there?"

"Sarah," he said. "She didn't mix in with the bunch. All she did was sit and watch. Shanks is some kind of a sadist, I guess. The only times he looked happy was when he was beating the bejesus out of somebody else."

"You figure Broderick knew about you and Melanie?"

"No chance," he said confidently. "Sarah did, maybe."

"Would she have told her brother?"

"How the hell would I know?"

"Maybe she would," I said slowly. "If she figured it was to her advantage."

"I guess you're right," he said.

"According to Sarah, Melanie flaunted her wanton affairs with other men right under Broderick's nose," I said.

"So she knew about me and Melanie," he said easily.

"How do you feel about Melanie?"

"She's a nice girl," he said. "Real good in the hay. And uncomplicated, too. I like that in a woman."

"Maybe you liked her too much," I said. "With Broderick out of the way you get Melanie, and her share of his estate, which is all wrapped up in your motel and canal complex, you tell me."

"You know something, Boyd?" He grinned lazily. "That's what I'd call getting Melanie the hard way!"

"Maybe you're right," I said in a grudging voice. "Where did Charles Gray figure in this?"

"He's their attorney," he said. "He makes out the

contracts, punches in the dotted lines, gets everybody to sign in the right places and he's happy."

"You make him sound like a real simple character," I said.

"I figure him for an educated son of a bitch," Adams said. "His problem was he was never educated how to make money. My guess is it riles him something real bad."

"Bad enough for him to try and do something about it?"

"You keep right in there, prodding," he said. "I wouldn't know, Boyd. I got me this little old country boy lawyer right here who knows the local background real well. Any contract Gray gives me to sign, it goes to my little old country lawyer first for him to check out. And if he says it's okay, then I send it up to my big city lawyer boy in San Francisco, and if he also says it's okay, then I get around to signing it."

"They've never found any problem with the contracts from Gray?"

"Never," he said. "It's possible, mind you, that Gray also' paid attention when I told him the routes his contracts were going."

"I bet!" I said slowly.

"Guess there's nothing else I can tell you, Boyd," he said.

"You know I was with Melanie up at the cabin and we found his body there?"

"She done told me about that," he said. "It sounded real nasty. Him lying up on top of the chandelier with his throat cut, and all, dripping blood all the way down the front of her shirt. When those lights came on it must have been like waking up in a slaughterhouse."

"You've got a gift for the right phrase, Hy," I said.

"That chandelier was nine feet up from the floor. Why the hell would anybody want to put a body up on top of it?"

"Maybe they didn't." He shrugged quickly. "Maybe Broderick climbed up there all by himself."

"Why would he want to do that?"

He grinned amiably. "Why don't you figure it out for yourself, Boyd? I can't work out all your problems for you. It wouldn't be fair, right? Not with Melanie paying you good money to figure them out for yourself."

"Your chair is mickey-moused." I made a big production out of checking my watch. "Timed to self-destruct in two seconds from now!"

Adams leaped out of the chair like he had just been goosed by a scorpion. Five seconds went slowly by and then he exhaled loudly through his nose.

"I was just a-funning you, Hy," I said. "Kind of reminds me of the good old days back home when I was just a kid, knee-high to a hooker. My paw would hoist old grannie up by her heels and dunk her head in the rain barrel. Laugh! We nearly died right there along with old grannie."

He sat down again and glared at me ferociously. "You got a real lousy sense of humor, Boyd!"

The waiter reappeared and ignored me completely. He gave Adams a beaming smile and said, "Are you ready to have lunch now, sir?"

"I guess so," Adams said.

"Hold it!" I said. "Just what are we eating, exactly?"

"Brioche de foie gras, to start with," the waiter said. "Followed by roast duckling farci à la greque."

"You still having a problem getting that Greek ground wheat?" Adams asked casually.

"No, sir." The waiter smiled fondly at him. "We took your advice about that particular source of supply, I'm happy to say."

"No sherbert to follow?" I said sourly.

"Strawberries Romanoff to follow," the waiter said frostily, then smiled at Adams again. "The Dom Perignon is chilled, sir, if you approve."

"I approve," Adams said happily. "My friend here is paying the tab."

"When the tab comes, I think I'm going to kill you," I said from between my teeth.

"It's like I said, Boyd." He grinned broadly at me. "You got a real lousy sense of humor."

Chapter Eleven

~~~~~~

It was around four in the afternoon when I got back to town. My shirt was clinging to my back again, and I felt lousy. Even more lousy every time I remembered the size of the tab at the bay restaurant. I parked out front of the two-story frame house, then went inside. There didn't seem to be anybody minding the store, so I hollered "Gray!" at the top of my voice.

Charles Gray emerged from his office a few seconds later, with a disapproving frown on his face. He was impressive, I had to admit to myself—the neat black hair with the touch of gray at the temples, the deep tan, and the athletic stride. He looked so clean-cut you automatically figured he just didn't sweat.

"Oh," he said shortly. "It's you, Boyd. I might have known!"

"Your help's having a day off?" I asked him. "Mrs. Townsend, if that's her name?"

"Mrs. Townsend is away sick," he said. "I've had another lady helping out but she had to leave early this afternoon. What do you want, Boyd?"

"I'm trying to find out who killed Broderick Rigby," I said.

"Oh, yes." He sounded bored. "You told me that before, I remember. Melanie hired your professional services, is that right?"

"Right," I said.

"I mentioned it to Captain Schell later," he said. "He seemed to find it quite amusing."

"He's got a great sense of humor, the captain," I said. "I figured I'd find her myself without bothering you, Gray, but I was wrong about that. Where is she?"

"I have no idea what you're talking about, Boyd."

"Eleanor Townsend," I said. "Where is she?"

"I told you," he said patiently. "She's away sick. Has been for the last couple of days."

"I picked her up off the sidewalk right outside your office that morning," I said. "Persuaded her to play hooky for the day and pretend she had a migraine. We went up the coast and stayed at a motel. We had dinner in a restaurant, then went back to the motel. In the middle of the night somebody came into the room, knocked me out cold, then took her away. I know where she was last night. Now I want to know where she is today."

He shook his head slowly. "Are you feeling all right, Boyd?"

"Nobody followed us," I said. "I would have known if they had. It's a kind of professional training. You get a feel for it. Nobody followed us that day, but they knew exactly where to find us in the middle of the night. So she must have told somebody exactly where we were going. I'd already left it up to her and she knew it. She only made one phone call, Gray. To you. To tell you about her sudden migraine. But she also told you exactly where we were going."

"It has to be the heat," he said. "Either that, or you've had a sudden fit of insanity!"

"They beat the hell out of her last night until she fainted from the pain," I said. "They figure on doing the same to her tonight, and every night here on out unless I quit and get out of town. Doesn't that worry, you, Gray? They could wind up killing her!"

"The only advice I can offer you is, see a doctor," he said shortly. "Either that, or have yourself committed to the nearest asylum."

"They're crazy," I said. "The both of them. You know that!"

"If anybody's crazy around here, it's you, Boyd," he said, "and if you don't get out of here immediately, I'll call Captain Schell and file a complaint against you."

"Okay," I said. "I'll go."

"You honestly should see a doctor," he said in an almost kindly voice. "You don't look well, Boyd. Exhausted, if you don't mind me saying so."

"The pipes, the pipes are calling," I said.

"What?" He looked at me blankly.

"If you've got a name like mine," I explained, "you hear them from time to time."

I walked out of his office and back to the car. The pipes were calling, okay, I figured, but not for me. I drove out to Paradise Beach and parked the car out front of the cottage. Melanie opened the door a whole inch and peeked at me through the crack.

"Oh," she said. "It's you!"

She opened the door wider, revealing to my interested gaze that she was only wearing blue silk bikinis. Her heavy breasts with their pink aureoles looked me straight in the eye, and I resisted the temptation to wink back at them.

"I didn't want a man to see me like this," she confided. "It would have embarrassed me."

"What am I?" I growled. "Some kind of a eunuch?"

"You're some kind of family right now, I think," she said. "I wish you wouldn't ask me questions like that, Danny, because I only get confused."

I followed her into the living room, admiring once again the contours of her swaying buttocks, the cleavage between them still visible beneath the blue silk. In the room, I sat down on the couch.

"I was just out of the shower and thinking about getting dressed," she said. "When you rang the doorbell, I mean. You want a drink?"

"Yes," I said. "I want a drink."

She made me a drink, then brought it across to the couch, her full breasts bouncing freely as she walked.

"I had lunch with Hy Adams today," I said.

"I know," she said. "You made the appointment at a most inconvenient time last night, remember?"

"Did Broderick ever talk with you about his investments?" I asked her.

"Not much," she said.

"The motel and canal complex," I said. "The one Hy is building. Did Broderick ever talk about that?"

She wrinkled her nose thoughtfully. "He did mention it when we were orginally discussing the divorce settlement. Something about he couldn't afford the four hundred thousand because it would leave him flat broke. The rest of his money was tied up in the motel and canals deal, and he couldn't realize on it for the next couple of years." She shrugged. "I told him it was his problem."

I drank some of my drink and wished my back would stop hurting. Also my front, and especially between my legs.

"I guess I'd better finish dressing," she said brightly. "I'm expecting Hy to call any time now, and he just might get the wrong idea if he found us to-gether and me wearing practically nothing at all."

"Why don't you do that?" I said. "I'll get the door when he arrives."

"Thanks, Danny." She gave me a warm smile. "You know, sometimes you're a real nice guy."

"What do you and Hy have in mind for tonight?" I asked.

"Nothing special," she said. "I'm going to cook him dinner and then we're going to stay home and—well, you know!—there's just nothing like it to soothe my nerves."

"I remember," I said.

She went out of the room with her buttocks bouncing gaily under the thin blue silk, and I vaguely remembered—in between the twinges—what it was like to have been young. I sipped my drink, spacing it carefully, and around ten minutes later the doorbell rang. It took a little while to haul myself up off the couch, then I walked slowly to the front door and opened it.

"You're every-goddamned-where today, Boyd," Adams boomed. "Now you're beating my time with my girl, right?" He laughed heartily to make sure I appreciated he had just made a big joke.

"One-million-five," I said, "and all Rigby family money, right?"

"What?" He stared at me for a moment, then grinned. "Oh, yeah. What we were talking about at lunchtime. Sure. All Rigby money, Boyd. I wanted to thank you for that lunch again, and—"

His voice trailed away into silence as I lifted the Magnum out of the shoulder rig, then pointed it at the glittering Cadillac Eldorado parked out front.

"Oh, no!" he whimpered. "Not the gas tank again."

"And it was all Rigby money, right?" I said in a snarling voice.

"Well, it was mostly Rigby money," he said. "Like, better than a million was Rigby money."

"And the rest?"

"Well, Charles Gray cut himself in for a piece."

"How big a piece?"

"Four hundred thousand, to be precise," he said, then swallowed hard. "I didn't figure it was important. Honest!"

"I know," I said wearily, and put the gun back into the rig. "You're just a simple country boy."

We went into the house, and I sat down on the couch again and generously allowed him to make me another drink.

"If you don't mind me asking," he said cautiously after he had given me the drink, "what's it all about, Boyd?"

"My guess is Gray used Rigby money for his share of the action," I said, "but he never bothered about telling them."

"And?"

"And maybe Broderick found out. He needed money to make a divorce settlement, remember?"

"You mean Gray killed him to keep his mouth shut?" Adams said, then swallowed hard again. "Jesus!"

"It wouldn't be Gray's style to do it himself," I said. "He'd get somebody else to do it for him."

"Like who?"

Melanie came bouncing back into the room, wearing a bright cotton number in a brilliant yellow.

"Hello, Hy," she said. "I hope you two guys are

being polite to each other. You look like you're getting along together just fine."

"He was going to mickey-mouse my gas tank again," Adams said gloomily. "He just isn't right in the head. I don't know why the hell you hired him in the first place."

"If you can put a cat among the pigeons," I said slowly, "I don't see any reason why you can't put a pigeon among the cats."

"Whatever it is," Adams said quickly, "I don't want any part of it."

"Me neither!" Melanie said, even more quickly.

"You want to know who killed Broderick, right?" I said reasonably. "So you can pick up that half million that's coming to you from his will."

"Wrong," she said coldly. "I want *you* to find out who killed Broderick. Forgive me for mentioning it, Danny, but that's why I hired you. That's why I'm paying you good money! I don't want any part of it."

"She's right, Boyd," Adams said. "I mean, it's none of my cotton-picking business, but she's right."

"Okay," I said, "but it's a shame."

"I know I'm going to hate myself for asking," Melanie said slowly, "but what's a shame, exactly?"

"Whoever killed Broderick can't inherit from his estate," I said. "Right?"

"Right," she said reluctantly.

"If we could prove it was Sarah who killed him, she couldn't inherit, right?"

"I guess so," Melanie said in a strangled voice.

"So he left his estate to you, his wife, and any surviving members of his family," I said, "which is Sarah. If she can't inherit because she murdered him, it leaves just you. A million dollars." I shrugged. "But

I'm not about to argue with you, honey. I understand your feelings. You just don't want to be involved."

There was a short, awkward silence, then Adams cleared his throat carefully.

"Like I said, it's none of my cotton-picking business," he said in an elaborately casual voice. "But, well—"

"A million dollars?" Melanie said, and choked on the words. "What do I have to do, Danny?"

"What do you both have to do," I corrected her. "The million is all tied up in Hy's development project, remember. So it's a group project."

Adams cleared his throat again carefully. "Just tell us what the both of us have to do, old buddy," he said.

"You each make a phone call," I said. "But it'll need a little rehearsal first for the both of you."

Maybe a half hour later, Melanie made the first call to Sarah Rigby.

"Look," she said coldly. "I know how we feel about each other, Sarah, but this can affect the both of us. Boyd's arranged a secret meeting with Gray up at the cabin for eight tonight. They're going to make a deal, and it means both of us will get screwed on the arrangement. So we have to be there to stop them going through with it. And bring that Townsend woman along with you, she's part of it."

Then she hung up and looked at me as her hands began to shake.

"How was I, Danny?"

"Just great," I said. "Now it's your turn, Hy."

He called Charles Gray at his home, and I wondered as his voice turned pure cracker-barrel.

"Hy Adams here, Mr. Gray," he said jovially.

120

"Mighty sorry to intrude on your evening but something's come up you should know about, I figure. Yes, sir! I guess you know me and Melanie Rigby are—well—you know!" He boomed with laughter. "Between a couple of gents like us, I guess I don't need to say any more. But this little girl trusts me, and I'm worried, to be real honest with you. She's going up to that cabin in the hills tonight around eight for some kind of a secret meeting. Well, like I said, that little girl confides in me. It's organized by that Boyd feller, and I don't trust him at all. All I know is, she's going to be there along with Sarah Rigby, and it's something about the money in poor old Broderick's estate not being quite right. I was sure amazed when I heard her talking with Sarah Rigby a while back. Like they was thicker than thieves, as my old grandpappy used to say! Well, I just figured you should know, Mr. Gray. I mean, I just wouldn't want anything to upset our project right now, because it's at a real delicate stage. Like it would be hard to realize a dime on the dollar if anything turned sour." He listened for a moment and the grin widened on his face.

"Yes, sir, Mr. Gray," he said. "Eight o'clock is the time for when the meeting is fixed. You'd do me a big favor with little old Melanie if you kind of forgot to mention it was me who told you about it." He listened for a few moments then said, "Any time, Mr. Gray. Any time at all!" Then he hung up.

"How was I?" he asked triumphantly.

"Almost as good as Melanie," I said blandly.

"He bought it, okay," he said. "One thing worries me, Boyd. Suppose they get together on this between now and eight?"

"If you were Gray or Sarah," I said, "would you feel like getting together with the other one?"

"Okay," Melanie said. "So what happens now?"

"You cook us some dinner," I said, "while Hy makes me another drink."

Chapter Twelve

The three of us got to the cabin early, around a quarter of eight. I found the lights were working okay and switched them on, then we went inside. Melanie looked up at the chandelier and shivered suddenly.

"It gives me the creeps being back here," she said.

"Why don't you go into the kitchen, Hy," I said. "Leave the light off and keep your big ears active when they arrive."

"Sure," he said. "But we'll hear them coming, right?"

"Right," I said.

"There's some liquor in the kitchen," Melanie said. "I sure could use a drink right now."

"No," I said. "It's not that kind of a party."

"A million dollars," she said. "Who needs it!"

"Now, honcy," Adams said quickly. "Don't be that way."

"We get along together just great in bed," she said. "So who needs a million dollars?"

"We could get married," he said, and swallowed hard.

"Married?" Her eyes lighted up. "Hy! You mean it?"

"Of course he means it," I said, "and I hope the three of you will be very happy."

"The three of us?" Adams mumbled.

"You, Melanie, and the motel and canals complex," I said. Then I heard the sound of a car approaching. "And you get in the kitchen, Hy."

"You want me to listen," he said doubtfully. "Is that all?"

"If things get rough you can rush in here with a gun in your hand," I told him.

His face paled under the heavy tan. "I don't have any gun!"

"Well, rush in anyway and shout 'Bang! Bang!'" I growled. "It should confuse them, at least!"

The car came to a stop outside and Adams moved toward the kitchen real fast. Maybe ten seconds later the door opened and Sarah Rigby walked in. She was followed by Shanks and Eleanor Townsend. Eleanor's face was gray with pain and she shuffled along like a little old lady. My whole body twinged in sympathy because I knew exactly how she felt.

Sarah came to a stop and looked at Melanie. "All right," she said in a brittle voice. "Where is Charles Gray?"

"He hasn't arrived yet," I said easily, "but he'll be along any time now."

"I didn't ask you, Boyd," she said. "I asked her!"

"The big development," I said, "the golden chance to get in on it alongside Adams. How much money did you put in, Sarah?"

"It's none of your goddamned business," she said tightly. "We're leaving right now, Bobo. And if Boyd tries to stop us, kill him."

"How much?" I said.

"Maybe you should tell him, Sarah," Shanks said hesitantly.

"All right." She stared at me down the length of her aristocratic nose. "Six hundred thousand dollars."

"How about Broderick?" I said.

"A half million," she said.

"The total investment was one-million-five," I said. "Charles Gray put in four hundred thousand."

"Don't be ridiculous!" she said scornfully. "He doesn't have that kind of money."

"Broderick did," I said, "and he never was that interested in investments. He left it all to you, right?"

There was the sound of another car approaching the cabin. Sarah put her lower lip between her teeth and nibbled on it gently.

"I don't believe it," she said finally.

"Maybe Broderick found out," I said. "If he did, it would be a good reason for killing him. Or having him killed."

The car came to a stop outside, and the silence grew expectantly. Then Charles Gray walked briskly into the cabin and came to a sudden stop when he saw the group already gathered.

"Boyd here says you invested four hundred thousand dollars of your own money in the Adams' development," Sarah said in a brittle voice. "I told him it was ridiculous, because you simply don't have that kind of money."

"And you were absolutely right," Gray said calmly. "Is this more of Boyd's hysterical accusations? He came into my office this afternoon and made the most idiotic suggestions that I—"

"There's one easy way to find out," I said. "We can always ask Adams."

"How do you suggest we do that?" Gray said, his voice heavy with sarcasm. "Employ a carrier pigeon?"

"Hy!" I raised my voice. "Come out here."

Adams appeared from the kitchen with a nervous grin on his face.

"Tell us about the investment money," I said pleasantly.

"Sure thing." He cleared his throat carefully. "One-million-one from the Rigby family, and four hundred thousand from Mr. Gray here."

"I see," Sarah said slowly, then looked at Gray. "Where did you get the money from?"

"It was a loan," Gray said quickly. "I would have repaid Broderick as soon as the investment was realized."

"There's one thing you should always remember when you borrow money, Charles," she said softly. "Always ask the lender first!" Her eyes glittered fiercely as she stared at him. "So that was why you killed my brother? Because he found out you had embezzled the money from him."

"Don't be stupid!" Gray said. "I never killed your brother."

"Then who did?" she snapped.

"He arranged a meeting with Melanie here that evening to talk about the divorce settlement," I said. "He told you about it, right?" Sarah nodded briefly. "Did he say why?"

"He was very excited," she said. "I thought it was nonsense, and I told him so." She looked at Melanie contemptuously. "That stupid bitch only wanted one thing and that was as much money as she could possibly gouge out of him."

"You told Shanks about it," I said, "and Gray?"

"I was concerned," she said. "I told his best friend and his attorney, yes."

"There was no car here when we arrived," I said, "only his body up on the chandelier. Somebody must have driven him up here."

"It wasn't me," Sarah said, and sniffed loudly.

"But it was you, Sarah," Gray said softly. "You, and your best friend, Bobo."

"You killed him, Charles, and you know it!" Shanks said tightly.

"I think we should all understand our various positions very clearly," Gray said icily. "Yes, I embezzled the money from Broderick. I was sick and tired of making fortunes for other people, and thought it was about time I made some money for myself. I intended to pay it back later, of course, one always does. But Broderick was worried about the divorce settlement and did some checking on his own. I had to stop him somehow."

"Charles." Shanks' lips drew back from his teeth in a fixed grimace. "This won't get us anywhere!"

"I think it will," Gray said. "Remember, I said we should all understand very clearly our relative positions in this. I'll even admit I lied to Broderick. I told him it had been done with his sister's connivance because she was so furious with him for ever marrying in the first place, after what they had been to each other."

There was a hissing sound as Sarah took a sharp breath.

"Broderick was in deep despair after I had told him," Gray continued in a completely neutral voice. "He said the only thing he could do was tell Melanie the whole truth and throw himself on her mercy. It was I who suggested he should meet her here secretly, at the place where they had spent their honeymoon. It was possible the surroundings would help his case with her, I suggested. Then, of course, I told Sarah exactly what he was about to do, but not why." He smiled cynically. "Everybody will understand that Sarah could never allow that to happen."

"I told him I understood," Sarah said, then laughed harshly. "Told him it would be better if Bobo and I went with him. The three of us could do a more effective job of persuasion than he could on his own. Broderick believed me. He always was an incredulous fool! Even if I did love him."

"Sarah, for God's sake!" Shanks said in an anguished voice. "Think what you're saying!"

"It makes no difference now," she said indifferently. "If I don't tell them, Charles will. So we brought him up here to the cabin early, and then we killed him. We knew Melanie would arrive later and find his body, and we hoped the police would believe she had killed him. But, unfortunately for us, she had to go and hire this fool, Boyd, here, to go with her."

"Tell me one thing," I said. "How did his body get up onto the chandelier?"

"I gave him a needle before we arrived," she said calmly. "We had experimented with drugs quite a lot before he married." She shook her head slowly. "Broderick was so stupidly trusting! I told him it would calm his nerves and he believed me. What I gave him was a large dose of stimulants. By the time we arrived, he just couldn't keep still. He was jumping about all over the place, with all his reflexes off, which was what we wanted in the first place, of course. But he almost went berserk. We just couldn't keep up with him. Then he bet us he could jump onto the chandelier and we bet him he couldn't. So he did it. I never saw anything like it in my life! He made this incredible running jump and landed on top of the wheel. His weight smashed most of the lightbulbs and he didn't even notice. But then he must have got some kind of a shock, because his body kept jumping convulsively and just wouldn't stop. So then Bobo got the knife from the kitchen and brought it back in here. He reached up and started sawing away at Broderick's throat. There was nothing Broderick could do about it, with the electric current still convulsing his body. Fortunately for Bobo, the knife had a wooden handle so he didn't get any shock." She looked across at Shanks' stunned face and smiled slowly. "Afterward, Bobo was ecstatic. It was his greatest experience ever, he said. He felt he'd somehow spent all his life building up to the ultimate experience. He said he'd never known such sexual ecstasy as the orgasm he had when the serrated knife bit into Broderick's throat and the blood spurted out."

"Stop it!" Melanie said in a shaking voice. "For God's sake, somebody stop that woman!"

"It's like I said," Gray said calmly. "We should all consider our respective situations. "I'm a self-confessed embezzler and—"

"—And a party to a coldblooded murder before the event," I finished for him.

"That, too," he said softly. "While Sarah and Bobo are self-confessed murderers. So what are we going to do?"

Shanks took a gun out of his pocket and held it firmly. "I'm going to walk out of here and nobody's going to stop me!"

"Very unenterprising, Bobo," Gray said. "Who is expendable here? Boyd, obviously, for a start. And Mrs.

Townsend." He gave Eleanor a wintry smile. "You shouldn't have changed horses in mid-stream, my dear. You were supposed to be on my side. We gave you a free entry to all the orgies so you could safely indulge your sexual promiscuity, and also maintain your facade of respectable widowhood. It was very foolish of you to be so taken with Boyd that you had to give him some real leads."

"What are you trying to say, Charles?" Sarah asked harshly.

"From what you told me, they're both badly marked," he said. "Perhaps in an excess of masochistic ecstasy they could even kill each other?"

"Or one could kill the other, then commit suicide in a fit of remorse," Sarah said briskly. "It still leaves Melanie and Adams."

"I'm sure they'll see things our way," Gray said in an almost paternal voice. "See where their true interests lie. If all this comes out, Adams' project will be ruined, and him along with it, I shouldn't be surprised. And I think Melanie should know that if the Adams' project sinks, all her hopes of any kind of inheritance sink along with it. Every cent Broderick has is already invested in the project. But if she goes along with us, she'll inherit her half million, and probably more when the investment is realized."

"I guess," Adams said, then cleared his throat carefully, "we were never here. So I'll take Melanie back home with me right now."

"You bastard!" Melanie said in a low voice. "You'd just walk out of here and leave Danny and Mrs. Townsend to be murdered?"

Adams shrugged broadly. "It's like the man says, honey, if the deal is ruined, then the both of us are ruined. I wouldn't like that, and neither would you. You coming, honey?"

"You can get fucked!" she said passionately.

"Okay." Adams shrugged again. "I guess if you don't want to take the chance you've been offered, they'll think of something else for you."

He started walking slowly toward the door, keeping his gaze fixed on the floor. When he came up beside Shanks, he made a sudden lunge for the gun. It wasn't the most expert lunge in the world. He managed to get a grip on Shanks' wrist and push his hand to one side, and, at the same moment, Shanks' finger involuntarily tightened on the trigger and the gun exploded. Sarah Rigby went backward, her eyes wide with disbelief as the blood started to spurt from her chest. Then Shanks threw off Adams' grip and swung the gun back toward him. By that time I had the Magnum in my hand and I fired a couple of shots in quick succession. Both of them took Shanks high in the chest, knocking him off his feet. More blood spurted. And then it was all over.

"Hy!" Melanie flew into his arms. "My hero! Will you ever forgive me for believing you were going to be the kind of bastard you were pretending to be!"

"Sure, honey," he said. "For a real nasty moment there, I almost had myself believing it."

"Very touching," Gray said dryly. "Well, I'm glad it's all over. I expect you feel the same, Boyd?"

"All over," I said. "For you?"

"The murderers have been uncovered and have met their just deserts," he said. "It's all finished, Boyd."

"It will be when I hand you over to Captain Schell," I said.

"I wouldn't do that if I were you," he said softly.

131

"The way things are now, everybody stands to benefit. Expose me, and you bring the whole development project crashing around your ears. Adams is ruined, and your client will inherit nothing, Boyd. And that will mean you won't get paid your fee, I imagine!"

I thought about it for a while then shrugged. "I guess you're right," I said reluctantly.

"I'm always right," he said. "I think I'll leave now. I'm sure you'll find a suitable explanation of everything for Captain Schell."

"I guess so," I said.

"Danny!" Melanie looked at me, wide-eyed. "You're not going to let him get away with it!"

"It's like he said," I told her, "I don't have any choice."

"Good night." Gray smiled faintly at me, then turned on his heel and started walking toward the door.

I let him get about six paces away from me, then said, "Gray!" He turned around toward me and must have seen it in my eyes. He opened his mouth to plead, or maybe protest, but I didn't wait to find out. I pulled the trigger of the Magnum and shot him between the eyes. As if miraculously, the hole appeared on his forehead, and then as the slow tumble of blood, brains, and sundry gore began to seep out of it, he collapsed to the floor.

"Danny?" Melanie said weakly.

"It was like he said," I told her, "he didn't leave us any choice."

"I'm glad you killed him," she said. "But how are you going to explain it?"

"I'm not," I said.

"What?"

"Somebody will find their bodies before long," I said. "Schell is bound to start looking when he hears the three of them are missing. And, for sure, he'll look up here." I wiped the butt clean with my pocket handkerchief, then held the gun by the barrel. Then I kneeled down beside Sarah's body and put the gun in her hand, clasping her fingers firmly around the butt.

"What's that going to prove?" Melanie asked.

"She shot Gray and Shanks," I said. "Shanks shot her. Schell can figure it out from there, that's what he's paid for."

"But it's your gun," Adams said huskily.

"Sure," I said, "but not the gun that's registered with the police. It's an old private detective's dirty trick. If you figure you need to carry a gun because you might also need to use it, you don't carry your official gun. That one's strictly unofficial and has never been on record any place. It cost me a lot of money, and now I guess the replacement is going to do the same."

"So none of us say anything," Adams said. "What then, Boyd?"

"There's no scandal attached to the project, so it goes ahead, I guess," I said. "Melanie will inherit all of Broderick's estate, and some lucky bastard will inherit the four hundred thousand stake in the project from Gray's estate. But I guess there's nothing we can do about that."

"Who's complaining?" Adams said, and grinned slowly.

"Schell will come sniffing around like a terrier," I said. "The four of us will need an alibi for tonight."

"It won't be any problem for me and Hy," Melanie said, almost happily. "The only time we got out of

bed tonight was to eat dinner, then we got right back in again!"

"How about you and Mrs. Townsend?" Adams asked.

"I guess we can arrange something between us," I said easily.

Melanie and Adams dropped us at the Paradise Beach cottage, and I picked up my own car there, then drove back to Eleanor's house. I parked the car a couple of blocks away because I didn't want the neighbors remembering the time it arrived at the house. Then we walked back to her house like real slow.

She made us both a drink, then sat in an armchair facing me as I sat on the couch, and smiled slowly.

"Our alibi is going to be the same as theirs, right?" she said.

"Right," I agreed.

"All he said about me was true," she said steadily. "The pure little widow-lady, a paragon of virtue, and all the time I was loving every vicious moment of those orgies up at Bobo's house."

"I don't know what you expect me to do," I said plaintively. "Bust out crying, or what?"

"You're a miserable cynical bastard, Danny Boyd," she said. "You know that!"

"I'm tired," I said. "Killing people always makes me feel tired."

"You had no choice," she said quietly. "I admired you for it, Danny. If I've got to fall for a bastard, I always prefer a genuine one."

I finished my drink, got up off the couch, and walked stiffly into the bedroom. It took a while to strip off my clothes, then I limped into the shower and turned the faucet on. After I had dried myself off tenderly, I shuffled back into the bedroom. Eleanor was standing there naked in front of the mirror. She turned around as I came into the room, then her shoulders started to shake.

"Look at the both of us!" she gurgled. "Like raw meat in a butcher's shop!"

I pulled back the covers and stretched out very carefully on the bed. She switched off the lights a few seconds later, then lay down beside me.

"I know it's ridiculous," she said softly, "but I'd feel a hell of a lot better facing Captain Schell if I knew our alibi was true."

"True?" I grunted.

"True," she said. "I mean, the way Melanie and Hy Adams' alibi will be true."

Her fingers lightly touched my shaft, and I winced.

"Maybe it's not possible?" she said anxiously.

"Maybe you're right," I said.

Her fingers fluttered expertly and I felt a stirring twinge.

"This just isn't fair of me, is it, Danny?" she said. "I mean, I'm hurting you."

She suddenly came up on her knees, then her head went down and I felt the exquisite sensation as her tongue lapped my shaft into a proud, but painful, erection.

"Does it still hurt?" she asked nervously.

"Like hell," I said truthfully, "but don't stop."

A while later she straddled me, then gently lowered herself down onto my throbbing shaft.

"Ouch!" I yelped.

"I'm not hurting you, Danny?"

"No, everything is just fine," I said quickly. "How are things with you?"

"Just fine," she said. "*Ouch!*"

My old man was right about one thing, I figured, as we reached an ouching climax a few minutes later; where there's a will, there's a way!

Big Bestsellers from SIGNET

☐ **SAVAGE EDEN by Constance Gluyas.** (#J7171—$1.95)

☐ **ROSE: MY LIFE IN SERVICE by Rosina Harrison.**
(#J7174—$1.95)

☐ **THE FINAL FIRE by Dennis Smith.**
(#J7141—$1.95)

☐ **SOME KIND OF HERO by James Kirkwood.**
(#J7142—$1.95)

☐ **A ROOM WITH DARK MIRRORS by Velda Johnston.**
(#W7143—$1.50)

☐ **THE HOMOSEXUAL MATRIX by C. A. Tripp.**
(#E7172—$2.50)

☐ **CBS: Reflections in a Bloodshot Eye by Robert Metz.**
(#E7115—$2.25)

☐ **'SALEM'S LOT by Stephen King.** (#J7112—$1.95)

☐ **CARRIE by Stephen King.** (#E6410—$1.75)

☐ **FATU-HIVA: Back to Nature by Thor Heyerdahl.**
(#J7113—$1.95)

☐ **THE DOMINO PRINCIPLE by Adam Kennedy.**
(#J7058—$1.95)

☐ **IF YOU COULD SEE WHAT I HEAR by Tom Sullivan and Derek Gill.** (#W7061—$1.50)

☐ **THE PRACTICE OF PLEASURE by Michael Harris.**
(#E7059—$1.75)

☐ **ENGAGEMENT by Eloise Weld.** (#E7060—$1.75)

☐ **FOR THE DEFENSE by F. Lee Bailey.** (#J7022—$1.95)

THE NEW AMERICAN LIBRARY, INC.,
P.O. Box 999, Bergenfield, New Jersey 07621

Please send me the SIGNET BOOKS I have checked above. I am enclosing $_____(check or money order—no currency or C.O.D.'s). Please include the list price plus 35¢ a copy to cover handling and mailing costs. (Prices and numbers are subject to change without notice.)

Name_____

Address_____

City_____State_____Zip Code_____
Allow at least 4 weeks for delivery

More Big Bestsellers from SIGNET